Koren's Omega Neighbor

Draco International #2

An MM/MPreg Shifter Romance

by

A.J. Stone

Koren's Omega Neighbor (Draco International 2)
Copyright © September 2018 by A.J. Stone
Print ISBN: 978-1-942414-53-7

Editor: Nicoline Tiernan
Cover Artist: Nicoline Tiernan

Published by Lost Goddess Publishing LLC

This book is a work of fiction. While reference might be made to actual historical events or existing locations, the names, characters, places and incidents are either the product of the author's imagination or are used fictitiously, and any resemblance to actual persons, living or dead, business establishments, events, or locales is entirely coincidental.

Warning: This book contains sexually explicit scenes and adult language and may be considered offensive to some readers. It is not meant for underage readers.

About Koren's Omega Neighbor

Chayton Sadler wasn't looking for love in Verdance. The minute after he fulfilled the terms of his uncle's will, he planned to be back home with his pack of black Labs.

Koren Tafari wasn't looking for love, but from the moment he set eyes on the sexy canine shifter and his dragon purred, he knew his number was up. Rather than fight it, he vowed to make Chay fall in love with him.

Some things are easier said than done, especially when his former mentor returns and is now an adversary threatening everything Koren holds dear.

Welcome to Draco International, home of high-powered dragon shifters who live by their own rules. This 44,000-word MPreg novel includes passionate and explicit sexual content, as well as some violence. Suitable for adult audiences.

Prologue—Chay

"Chay? You have to do it."

Chayton Sadler the Fifth scowled at his brother, a bit of his natural stubbornness coming to the fore. "I don't have to do anything I don't want to do."

Basil's usual grin was absent. His somber brown eyes regarded Chay with more than a little sympathy. "We all have to jump through hoops. It's six months. You can survive in the city for six months."

Chay's scowl didn't lessen. "You're saying just that because you get to go to the country house. Living out on a private ranch for six months isn't a hardship. You can shift whenever you want and roam free. I have to move to Verdance, which is a fairly large city. In a city, people are always around. I'm giving up my freedom, my independence, and my morning run."

Growing up near a nature preserve had been wonderful for the family of black Lab shifters. Their nearest neighbors were ten wooded acres away, affording Chay and his siblings the freedom to shift as often as they wanted. Chay spent a lot of time in canine form. It was part of his core identity.

Basil slung an arm around his littermate. "There was no provision against you going to a park and running free for a while."

"Dog parks in the city require an owner to be present. I'll bite anyone who tries to own me." Chay's dry tone kindled a chuckle from his brother.

"I bet you would."

"Plus, I won't get to see you. I can't remember ever going longer than a day or two without seeing you." A bit of a whine infused his tone. He couldn't help it. Twenty-four years ago, he and Basil had been birthed into the Sadler family.

They were the second litter for their fathers. They had an older brother and two sisters. Being part of a large family meant that Chay was used to having his pack around him at all times. He'd even commuted to community college because he hadn't wanted to be

1

away from his family, and he'd eschewed a higher degree because it would mean he'd have to leave home. Also, he couldn't figure out a career path, and going to school just to accumulate credits seemed like a waste of time.

His sisters and brother had moved out, but they lived nearby. The entire family got together at least twice each week, and not a day passed that someone didn't drop by for a visit.

Basil drew him closer for a hug. "That's what makes this hard for me, Chay. Maybe I'm going to a ranch, but none of you will be there. I'll be a ten-hour drive away from here, and a twelve-hour drive from you."

Chay rested his head on his brother's shoulder. "Bas, let's say no. Let's refuse."

"It's not about just us." Basil's voice dropped to a desolate whisper. "If we don't do this, nobody gets their inheritance."

"It's not fair."

Not fair was the terms of a distant uncle's will. Chayton Sadler the Second had died without heirs, so he'd left everything to his namesake's brood—and he'd slapped some serious conditions upon that inheritance. Chay's omega father—Chayton Sadler the Fourth—had been named after his father's uncle, and he'd passed the name to his youngest son. This uncle had been tickled and pleased and all that kind of thing. To show his appreciation, he'd left his millions to Chay's father—provided Chayton the Fifth and Basil, whose name he'd suggested, each inhabited one of his far-flung properties for six months.

Basil would live on a secluded ranch, and Chay would be stuck in an apartment in the midst of a busy city.

At the end of six months, Chayton Sadler the Second's vast wealth would be evenly split among his fathers and siblings. Money like that was life-changing, and neither Chay nor Bas had settled on a path in life.

Always the voice of reason, Basil reminded Chayton of the reasons they had to do this for their family. "No, it's not fair, but Dad needs a hip replacement, and Father's been worrying a lot about not having enough saved up to retire. Cole has that dream of opening up a wildlife refuge with Felicity and Bette."

Their parents' needs were more pressing and enough of a reason. From the moment he heard the terms of his distant uncle's will, Chayton knew he'd fulfill the terms. He just hated the idea of being away from everyone he held dear.

"Promise you'll make the best of it," Basil added.

"Let's go for one last run." Chay shed his clothes and shifted into a large black Labrador retriever.

Basil followed suit. Where Chay was completely black, Bas had white on two of his paws.

Chay took off, a burst of speed putting him out front, but Bas caught up before long.

This was the life he loved.

Chapter 1—Chay

Running under the cover of night was strangely exhilarating. Nobody was around, and Chay had the park to himself. His clothes were stowed in a small backpack hidden in a cluster of bushes that retained the faint odor of marijuana. The teens who'd been camped out there were long gone.

He spent some time sniffing, getting to know the lay of the land and the marking of various territories. Tonight was his tenth night sneaking out for a 4 am run, and he was feeling a little reckless, so he veered out of the park to explore the city streets. When the first streaks of light appeared on the distant horizon, he headed back to the park, shifted, and hurriedly dressed.

Then he jogged back to the high-rise in the expensive part of town where Great-Uncle Chayton was making him live for the next 172 days. The doorman, a woman, opened the door and nodded to him. "Good morning, Mr. Sadler."

"Morning, Courtney."

A different doorman had been on duty when he'd left. This was another advantage of his early morning jog—it coincided with shift change. Nobody could definitively track his comings and goings.

"Chayton Sadler V."

Chay stood in the lobby of the upscale apartment building. Someone saying his name drew his attention toward the row of mailboxes accessible by a tiny key he had yet to find.

The person in question had broad shoulders that were almost swallowed up by a mane of shaggy hair. His strong physique tapered to trim hips that had Chay looking closer. Long legs, long torso—this man was seriously tall. At six feet, Chay was not a small man, but next to this guy, he felt downright tiny.

Though the guy wore a wrinkled dress shirt with jeans, he didn't seem as out of place as Chay felt in the elegant main floor of his uncle's building.

"It's 'the fifth,'" Chay supplied. "Not 'V.'"

At the sound of his voice, the man turned. Clear, blue eyes regarded Chay with an intense sense of bafflement. "You're Chayton Sadler the Fifth?"

"Yeah. That's me." Chay had been in the building for a week, and he'd met a few neighbors. Most were professionals who were too wrapped up in their work to appreciate the luxurious amenities this place had to offer.

The bonus features didn't make up for not being at home with his pack, though. No hot tub, swimming pool, fitness room, tennis court, or restaurant could replace easy access to his fathers and siblings.

But the power of this mystery man's penetrating perusal made him forget to be homesick for the moment.

The man held up a stack of envelopes, but his gaze devoured Chayton's body. "You don't live in 14A."

Confusion made Chay slow to respond. Or maybe he should be outraged? Sure, he didn't dress in tailored suits, but neither did this hunk of gorgeous man. "It was my uncle's place. He passed away last month, and I inherited it."

The man's lips pressed together, but he appeared puzzled, not angry. "I live in 14A, and a female couple lives in 14B." He hooked his thumb through a belt loop, drawing attention to his loose-fitting jeans. One well-placed tug, and they'd probably slide right off. "What floor are you on?"

Chay frowned. "Fourteen. The elevator guy always takes me to fourteen."

Each floor held two apartments, neatly labeled A or B.

The guy held out the stack of mail. "You live in 13A, directly below me. The addresses here are off by one floor because the ground floor is called 'Main' and the second floor is called 'one'. Someone who didn't understand how numbers work made up the addresses."

Chay reached for the stack, and his hand brushed the handsome neighbor's mighty paw. A charge ran through him, and the dog part of him let loose with a subsonic whine.

The man stilled. That knowing gaze probed the depth of Chay's eyes for something. Time seemed to stand still with that handsome face frozen in a frown. Chay had the opportunity to note the light brown stubble staining the man's tanned skin and the tiny laugh lines around those entirely kissable lips. He wondered what it would be like to run his fingers through that mop of hair and what it would feel like for that stubble to scratch across his stomach.

This guy had to be almost twice his age. He was closer to Chay's fathers' ages than Chay's, but right now, Chay couldn't seem to care.

The years melted away, and his canine let loose another subsonic whine.

Releasing his hold on the mail, the guy took a step closer, his nose twitching as he—was he *sniffing* Chay? This dude was a canine shifter? Given his size, he had to be a Great Dane or an extra-large Pyrenees.

Chay squared his shoulders and straightened his posture. He kept his gaze glued to his upstairs neighbor. When the guy took another step closer, Chay backed up. "I didn't catch your name."

A rumbling came from deep in the man's throat. Was he purring? Maybe he was a cat shifter, maybe a panther or lion. Fuck—that meant he was dangerous. But he didn't seem like he was unstable. "Koren Tafari."

Tafari rhymed with safari, so maybe Koren was a lion shifter. Lions were known for being unpredictable, territorial, and they had violent tempers. Or he was way off. Maybe this guy was just strange.

Even if he was a shifter, Koren's intensity meant he was focused and possibly an apex predator. As a member of an easygoing breed, Chay could do without that kind of stress in his life. No matter how much his canine wanted to inhale Koren's delicious scent or rub his head against the man's side, he wasn't going to do it.

Chay stuck out a hand. "Hi, Koren. I'm Chay. It's nice to meet you. I'll get down to the post office first thing and get the address corrected. I'm sorry about the inconvenience."

Those blue eyes moved over his body, heat lasering away Chay's clothes and leaving no doubt as to the content of the older man's thoughts. "It's not an inconvenience. You're new to the city?"

The deep timbre of his voice rumbled through Chay's body, leaving a yearning shiver in its wake.

"Yeah. I grew up about twelve hours away." He meant to glance around the elegant lobby, but he found it impossible to break the hold Koren had over him. "I'm still figuring out where things are."

"You're a jogger?" Somehow, Koren managed to move closer, and Chay was just now noticing. He fingered the strap of Chay's backpack. "How far are you planning to go?"

By Chay's calculations, he'd covered at least a dozen miles. "I went already. I got a couple hours in."

Koren's brows lifted. "A serious runner sweats."

Dogs panted, and Chay had barely broken a sweat in the mile between the park and the apartment. Meeting Koren's challenge, he chuckled. "Do they?"

Again, Koren's gaze moved over him. "What kind of shifter are you?"

Oh—so they were going to get it all out in the open now?

6

Chay didn't blink. "Lab."

Koren grinned, a careless, flirty expression with a hint of lust. "I've always had an affinity for larger breeds."

"What are you?" He hoped Koren wasn't a tiger or anything that might eat a dog.

"Dragon."

Lots of creatures shifted, but to Chayton's recollection, they were actual animals that existed as non-shifters. Dragons were fiction. Backing up, Chay held up a hand. "Like a Komodo dragon?"

"Sharp-Winged."

"There's no such thing as—"

"There he is!" A squeal had Chayton breaking off mid-denial.

He and Koren both turned to regard the interloper with no small degree of annoyance. The short, round woman didn't seem to notice.

Her eyes sparkled with joy, and she stuck out her hand. "You must be the new guy in 13A. I'm Lizz—two z's—Buika. I'm in 1B. I'm president of the advisory and welcoming committees."

"Hi, Lizz with two z's. I'm Chay Sadler. It's great to meet you." Chay shook her hand. Nothing about her seemed supernatural, so Chay figured she wasn't a shifter.

"Chay Sadler?" Frowning, she gazed in confusion. "Chayton Sadler passed away last month."

"He was my great uncle. I was named for him. He's Chayton Sadler the Second, and I'm the Fifth."

Her mouth opened the slightest bit, a rainbow trout suddenly finding itself lifted out of water. "The fifth? What happened to three and four?"

"My dad is four, and his cousin is three. When I have kids, I'll do a sixth, just to keep the name going. I'll call him Cha-cha."

She giggled and waved her free hand. "Oh, you. So handsome. I see you've already met our resident mad scientist. Koren, are you just getting in?"

The smolder in Koren's gaze cooled considerably, but he still greeted Lizz warmly. "I was working."

Grabbing his arm, she clucked in disapproval. "You need to get out more. You'll be single forever if you spend your life locked in a lab."

At the utterance, the mischievous slant returned to Koren's smile. "Locked in a Lab. That sounds like fun."

Catching the innuendo, Chay choked on his saliva.

Koren slapped him on the back a few times, but mostly he rubbed circles that sent Chay's libido into overdrive. "You okay?"

"Fine," Chay said.

Even though he'd just been coughing into them, Lizz took both of his hands in hers. "Chay, I want to throw a welcome party to introduce you to the building. How about this Friday night at your place?"

Normally when a person threw a party for someone, they provided the venue. Chay wasn't quite certain how to react. For some reason, he glanced at Koren. "At my place?"

Koren pursed his lips. "It's so everyone can gawk at your stuff."

"Did you do this when you moved in?"

"I did," Lizz said. "I don't mind having the party at my place, but yours is so much bigger."

Chay couldn't quite think of a reason to refuse. "It's my uncle's stuff." He'd cleaned out some things, but there was still a lot left to go through.

"Even better." A smirk played around Koren's mouth. "Your uncle didn't socialize with anyone in the building."

No one in the building seemed to be all that social. So far, Lizz was the lone butterfly.

Chay's mind couldn't keep away from thoughts Koren. The man was a supernova—hot to the core. Dragons breathed fire. Maybe his core was made of the stuff. It would explain the intensity and the heat rolling from him and battering Chay on a cellular level.

Chay thought about what Basil would advise him to do. "How about Saturday night? That'll give me a little more time to get settled."

"Wonderful," Lizz clapped. "I'll deliver flyers to all the apartments. Koren, you're coming, right?"

He shrugged. "If I get back in time. I have a business trip planned." Then that molten gaze captured Chay's again. "Perhaps I can take you to lunch today?"

This was crunch time. If he refused, he was telling the shifter he had zero interest in him. If he went, then Chay would need to figure out what kind of interest he really had in this man who claimed to be a dragon shifter. Were they drawn together because they were two shifters adrift in a sea of humans? Was Koren after a quick hook-up?

Chay didn't do quick hook-ups. He wasn't a hound dog. His breed was steadfastly loyal. He inhaled a huge breath. Lunch didn't mean sex, though it could mean flirting with this handsome neighbor. He grinned. "Sure. Why not?"

Lizz whipped out her phone. "Let's exchange numbers so we can work out details."

Koren backed away. "I need to get a couple hours of sleep. I'll knock on your door at one."

When he disappeared down the hall where the elevators were located, Lizz sighed. "You are so lucky, Chay. That man is seriously dreamy. I have a thing for nerds."

Koren didn't seem like a nerd. He had an athletic build and bearing, as did most shifters.

"It's just lunch," he said. "Koren was being nice." Where he was from, the entire neighborhood got together for a party whenever anybody new came in from out of town, even for a visit. New neighbors were a rarity, and they were always welcomed with open arms.

Lizz shook her head. "Koren Tafari is not a nice guy." Then her eyes grew wide. "I don't mean he's mean or evil or anything, just that he avoids anything involving the welcoming committee or events we have so people in the building can get to know each other. It's not like he needs to network, not with his position as head of research and design at Draco International. He has plenty of friends."

She slapped her hand over her mouth.

"I talk too much," she mumbled behind her hand. "Gossip is my kryptonite. I gotta stop."

It was refreshing to meet someone who lacked artifice. Chay laughed, and Lizz's face reddened.

Chapter 2—Koren

Koren flopped onto his stomach and pulled the covers over his naked body. The moment he closed his eyes, an image of Chayton Sadler the Fifth biting his lower lip appeared.

In his one hundred and forty-two years, Koren Tafari had dated a lot of men. He'd even had a few serious relationships. His dragon had never once reacted the way it had to the Labrador retriever shifter. Yeah, his dragon had genuinely liked and appreciated many of his lovers, but it had never once yearned for a specific one.

And this one was quite young. In human years, Koren estimated that he looked like he was in his mid-forties. Chay couldn't be more than twenty-five at most. He had a fresh-from-the-farm innocence about him that even farmers lost by the time life handed them grownup responsibilities.

He imagined those large, chocolate eyes glazed with passion, and his dick lengthened. *Fuck.*

Rolling to his back, he took himself in hand and imagined stripping Chay's clothes off his body. He hadn't been sweaty, no doubt because he'd run in his canine form, and Koren had a hankering to see what Chay looked like in a lather.

He'd smelled delicious, the scent of his personal care products mixing with his unique sweet musk. Koren's nostrils flared, trying to summon the memory of that heady aroma.

The brief contact had set off an electrical storm of desire Koren had to work hard to conceal. Remembering it now took him to the point of no return. His balls drew up, and he came.

After cleaning up, he called his friend. Amaricio Granger had recently settled down with a canine shifter. Edgar morphed into a cute little Tibetan Terrier, though he was shy about doing it with others present. Recently Edgar had birthed three dragon-pup hybrids. The babes, two boys and a girl, were adorable, though they wouldn't shift for the first time until they reached puberty, so there was no telling what they'd shift into.

"I thought you were going home to sleep. Don't tell me you came up with another fucking idea." Amar answered his cell with a snarl.

Koren wasn't taken aback. Amar was a gruff man, and that was how he communicated concern. Of course, he was almost never gruff with Edgar. One look from those puppy-dog eyes, and Amar melted.

For the first time, Koren had an inkling as to what his buddy had gone through. "No. I met someone. My dragon purred. It's never purred before."

On the other end, Amar chuckled.

"Grange, don't be a dick. What the hell am I supposed to do?" Of all their friends, Amar was the only one who'd fallen head-over-heels in love with anyone. He'd been willing to give up his friends, family, and career to make a life with Edgar. Being a real friend, Koren wasn't inclined to make Amar choose between relationships.

After another few seconds of laughter, Amar sobered. "Go find your mate. Trust your dragon. It knows what it needs."

"We have a lunch date. Should I dress up?"

"For fuck's sake, Koren. You've been dating for over a century."

"But it hasn't mattered before now." For the first time in his life, Koren had pre-date jitters. How the hell was he supposed to get a few hours of sleep when thoughts of Chay occupied his mind?

"Look, I didn't change myself for Edgar. He knew what he was getting from the start."

Koren snorted. "You wear suits every day of your life. I wear jeans, and I'm not sure I have a shirt that doesn't have a stain on it." The only time he'd seen Amar out of a suit was when he was in his dragon form or when Edgar asked him to wear something else.

"Tell you what—I'll have Edgar pick you up something suitable. What time is your date?"

Koren felt bad. Edgar was at home with three babies. He didn't need more to do. "He doesn't have to go through any trouble."

"He'll love it. Edgar has been wanting to get his hands on your wardrobe for a long time. Brielle is there, and she can watch the babies." Amar seemed inordinately pleased. "Now, tell me what time you're meeting your mystery man."

"One."

"Does he have a name?"

"Chayton Sadler the Fifth." Koren didn't know why he said Chay's whole name, except that he wanted to embrace the entirety of everything that made up the man who made his dragon purr.

"The fifth?" Amar laughed again. "Tell me he doesn't spend his free time playing tennis."

As Chay was a dog shifter, he might very well like tennis balls. "He jogs. He just moved into the apartment below mine, which he inherited when his uncle passed away. That's all I know."

"You'll know more after your date," Amar assured him. "I got to know Edgar slowly, and I liked the process. In a lot of ways, I'm still getting to know him."

Koren heard the satisfaction and peace in Amar's voice, and for the first time, he wanted to be tied down to one man. Koren craved a mate who would complete him.

Somehow he fell asleep because a knocking at the door roused him. Koren slid into a pair of jeans as he rushed to answer. He opened it to find Edgar holding several shopping bags and a short garment bag for dress shirts.

Edgar was a small man, about a foot shorter than Koren. His dark brown hair sported a blond patch above his right eye that was also there when he shifted. His dark brown eyes were lit by an effervescent inner glow, and his genuine smile stretched across his face. "I'm here, Koren, and I'm going to make you look fabulous, not that you need much help in that department."

Koren stepped aside to let Edgar breeze past him. The canine shifter was always full of energy, and sometimes being around him exhausted Koren. Chay seemed to have a quiet energy, which suited Koren much better.

Edgar sailed through the living room and into Koren's bedroom. "Where's your closet? I brought some stuff for today, but I wanted to get a handle on what else you have. We may need to do a complete wardrobe overhaul."

Ever since Edgar had stopped working at Draco International—he'd been Amar's personal assistant—he'd dropped the collared polo shirts and khakis in favor of bright colors that suited his style a lot better. Today he'd paired lemon yellow shorts with a pink-and-yellow-striped top. On his feet, he wore heavy sandals with thick straps to hold them in place.

Wondering what trouble he'd borrowed, Koren followed Edgar into the bedroom. "I was thinking I should wear jeans and a nice shirt."

Edgar huffed and parked his hands on his hips. "I've seen the way you dress, Koren. You have one suit, three pairs of jeans, and a dozen shirts. I don't even think you have shorts or sweats or anything to wear while you're relaxing."

As Koren often relaxed wearing nothing but a robe, he didn't comment.

Pulling open the closet door, Edgar went inside. The room was fairly empty when it came to clothes. Most shelves stored abandoned projects or geek-style collectibles.

Gasping, Edgar shook his head. "It looks like you've moved out and forgot to tell anyone."

"It's a big closet," Koren protested. "Nobody needs this many clothes."

Edgar grabbed a brown cassock. "Help me, Obi-Wan. You're my only hope."

"It was my costume last Halloween."

An ironic guffaw chuffed from Edgar. "It's your only Halloween costume. This year, you're doing something different, but that's a conversation for a different day—and maybe with a different man."

Whirling, Edgar pushed Koren back into the bedroom. "Okay, I bought several shirts of different styles, each appropriate to the occasion, and I bought you new jeans. Seriously, Koren—you have a nice ass. It's, like, a solid seven. You gotta show off your assets."

Koren blinked. "Does Amaricio know you've rated my ass?"

Edgar rolled his eyes. "Puh-leeze. You don't think I rated it by myself, do you? I gave you an eight, but Amar gave you a six. The seven was a compromise."

In addition to the items he mentioned, Edgar pulled out new socks, briefs, and shoes. The shoes were kind of cool. They had a constellation design, though Koren couldn't match them to any constellations he knew.

"Wow—you really went above and beyond. You didn't have to do this."

Looking him up and down, Edgar huffed. "Yes, I did. Amar said your dragon purred. I love when his purrs. It makes a sexy, rumbling sound that makes me want to lick him like he's covered in chocolate. Now, go shave, and jump in the shower as well. Wet down your hair so I can give you a trim. Even you have limits where the shaggy look is concerned."

Koren hurried because there wasn't a lot of time. When Edgar finished with him, he had a sleek haircut—he had to admit it looked better—and clean clothes. The jeans fit like a dream, with enough room in the crotch to accommodate his junk, but they were tight enough to show off his natural assets. He'd liked a number of the shirts Edgar had chosen, in his words, "to bring out the blue in your eyes." He ended up in a royal blue cotton shirt that had snaps halfway down the front.

Edgar undid the top three. "Where are you taking him?"

Given the eager excitement in Edgar's eyes, he hated to admit the truth. "Um, I hadn't thought about it."

"Amar took me to this intimate bistro that just opened up last week. It's called Petrichor, which is a strange word, but the food was scrumptious."

"It's the smell of rain."

"What?" Edgar smoothed the lines of Koren's shirt.

"Petrichor—it's the name of the smell of rain, usually after a period of warmth and dryness."

"Oh. Still a weird word. Anyway, they have great Italian bread there. When nobody was looking, Amar toasted mine with a little flame from his mouth, and it was really good. Also, the lobster bisque and the roasted chicken breast. That's what I had. Amar had steak because anytime we go someplace that serves steak, that's what he gets. I'm still working on getting him to live on the edge, maybe order some barbeque ribs or something." He chuckled in remembrance. "One day, he's going to eat a salad."

"Dragons are carnivores."

"You're half human, which makes you an omnivore. You need veggies in your life."

Koren checked out his reflection in the full-length mirror in the master bathroom. "I look good."

"Yes, you do." Edgar preened.

"Thank you for this. I owe you."

"Nah." Edgar waved his hand. "That's what friends are for. Plus, you helped save my life and stop the bad man from stealing my kids. So—this is nothing."

Chapter 3—Chay

Chay wasn't sure how much he should dress up for this lunch date. Koren hadn't seemed as uptight as most of the people in the building he'd encountered so far. His hair fell past his shoulders, and it bore evidence of a hand beating tracks through it repeatedly. Even his clothes made him seem like a guy who was extremely laid back. His jeans had been rumpled and stained. From the scents Chay had picked out, they hadn't been washed recently. The button-down shirt had been professional-looking at one time, but now it was wrinkled, untucked, and it had a lot of chocolate milkshake stains.

But then there were those intense eyes.

He called Basil.

"Chay, I miss you so much right now."

"Why? Are you okay?"

When Bas had arrived, he'd found it wasn't a ranch in name only. Uncle Chayton had a goat farm. He made cheese and yogurt. The property featured a row of cabins, each one occupied by a couple of ranch hands, and a larger house belonged to the manager.

Basil sighed. "I'm fine. I'm just homesick."

For the first time, Chay's primary emotion didn't involve missing home. "Have you made friends?"

The pair of them tended to make friends wherever they went. "I'm the boss's nephew, and since I'm set to inherit this place, they're still waiting to see if I'm going to continue running it or sell it off."

Chay winced because their plan had been to sell everything. However, employees meant other people's livelihoods were on the line.

"Enough about my troubles. What's going on in Verdance?"

"I have a date."

"Oh my God—you let me whine about things I can't change instead of leading with that? Tell me all about him. What's his name?"

"Koren Tafari. He's my upstairs neighbor, and we met by accident because he's been getting my mail. He's really tall, and he has broad shoulders."

Basil chuckled. "You've always been a shoulder guy."

Chayton liked strength, and he'd always been drawn to men with broad shoulders. "Yes, well, he's handsome. He's a little older, probably late thirties or early forties."

"Really? Is this like a Daddy thing?"

"No. I think he was surprised to find himself attracted to me." Chay paused and thought about what he was about to reveal. "He's a dragon shifter."

"He's a—what?" Basil scoffed.

"A dragon shifter." Chay wasn't sure he believed it himself. "He's huge, Bas, at least a whole head taller than me."

"But—a dragon shifter? That's fiction."

"I guess I'll see. My date is in an hour. I was calling you for advice about what to wear." He explained the way Koren had been dressed when they'd met.

Bas made a thoughtful sound. "Where is he taking you?"

"I didn't ask."

"Dumbass. Did you get his number?"

"No, and I'm not calling. He said he'd worked all night, and he needed a few hours of sleep before we went out. It's lunch, and it's the day-of, so no reservations are involved. Come on, Bas." Chay eyed a stack of jeans.

"What were you wearing when you met?"

"Um, a ratty T-shirt and black sweats."

"The ones with the white stripe down the side? I told you they were flattering."

Chay exhaled. "Yes. You were right. You're always right. Tell me what to wear."

"Go with those jeans we got last summer on our trip to the coast and your burnt orange collared shirt. It says you're trying, but not too hard." Bas exhaled. "Chay, be careful. You fall in love at the drop of a hat."

Chay felt his emotions very deeply. Perhaps he hadn't been in love all that much, but it had felt like it at the time. "I'll be careful," he promised.

At ten minutes after one, a knock sounded on the door. Chay checked his reflection in the mirror near the door one last time. As Basil had predicted, he looked great. That was the source of the satisfied smile he sported when he answered the door.

The smile grew as he took in Koren's appearance. "Oh, wow," Chay said. "You look—you look great." At the last moment, he reigned in his enthusiasm. Sometimes when he was excited, he could be overly effusive.

16

Koren's gaze moved over Chay's body, stripping him bare. The corner of his mouth tipped up in a half smile. He came through the threshold, closing the door behind him. "Thanks. So do you."

Automatically, Chay lowered his gaze as heat crept up his neck. Compliments always made him blush.

"Look, I wanted to tell you we're not the only shifters in the Verdance. Or in the building, for that matter. However, our presence here is still secret. Humans outnumber us by 200 to one."

Chay started, swinging his gaze up quizzically. "That's a lot of shifters in one place. Where I'm from, we have a few dog and cat shifters, and I knew one guy who was a fox shifter, but we kept it quiet. I know better than to broadcast my existence."

"I figured," he said. "I'm taking you to Petrichor. It's a new restaurant down the street. I haven't been there, but I have a friend who said the food was good."

Since his outfit was on par with what Koren was wearing, he didn't doubt his wardrobe. "Okay. Sounds great."

Before he could move, Koren's hand landed on Chay's arm. An electric shock ran through him, but instead of jumping away, he found himself leaning closer. Koren's lips brushed Chay's, and heat joined the electricity. With a small moan, Chay parted his lips, and Koren's tongue swept inside. Molten lava coursed through his veins and rendered his knees useless.

Chay sagged against Koren's body. The dragon shifter's hand moved to grip the back of Chay's neck, and his other hand spread over Chay's lower back, providing support and urging him closer. Chay clutched at Koren, snagging handfuls of his shirt.

Much too soon, Koren broke the kiss and put distance between them. He smoothed the wrinkles in his shirt. "I'm not going to pretend my dragon isn't really attracted to you."

Chay was still struggling with his reeling senses. "O—Okay."

"I'm an alpha." It was in his attitude, bearing, and the way he'd worded lunch plans.

Not a surprise. "I figured."

"And I'm significantly older than you. Before today, I'd never looked twice at someone as young as you."

Chay was aware of the age difference. "How much older?"

A wry smile twisted Koren's lips. "I'm one hundred forty-two years old."

"Oh." Chay sank down on a nearby ottoman. "That's really old. I'm only twenty-four."

"I figured." Koren infused irony into the words he parroted back to Chay. "If you don't want to do this, I'll understand."

"It's lunch," Chay said. "Just lunch." With a dragon shifter who was old enough to be his great-great grandfather. A sexy dragon shifter who lit fires in Chay's core and made him want to rub his naked body all over the alpha's.

The intensity in Koren's eyes quadrupled, and a fire smoldered behind them. "No, Chay. I'm trying to tell you this isn't just lunch. It's the beginning of a relationship. Dragons aren't like other shifters. When a dragon decides on a mate, it's for life, and my dragon wants you."

This sounded super serious. For the first time, Chay understood why some of his previous boyfriends had accused him of being too possessive or moving too fast. He was an emotional man, and he had always embraced his feelings. This time, he'd promised Basil he wouldn't rush into anything prematurely.

If a dragon was half as dangerous as a tiger, Chay could find his laid-back self in for a world of trouble. He was a little afraid. "You talk about your dragon like it's not part of you."

Koren slid another ottoman closer and parked himself in front of Chay. "When it comes to mystical matters, it's a separate entity. For instance, I would never in a million years have asked you out. While you're very handsome, you're incredibly young, and you're a dog shifter. I know absolutely nothing about you except that you like running in your dog form."

In the silence that followed, Chay noted the extreme care Koren had taken with his appearance. Though his hair was still down to his shoulders, the shagginess was gone. Now it looked stylish and chic. He'd shaved, and his clothes were clean. The jeans looked new, and the shirt delineated every sinewy muscle that made up his torso. The short sleeves emphasized the exceptional circumference of his biceps.

This date mattered to Koren.

Wetting his lower lip, Chay sought to control his nerves. "What if I don't feel the same way? I mean, about how serious this date is?"

Koren closed his eyes, severing a contact Chay hadn't known was so vital until that moment. "Your dog whined when it saw me, and my dragon purred. That means something."

"You're talking about fate, or predetermination." Chay rubbed his finger across his chin, but since he'd just shaved, his prickly calming device was missing.

"Perhaps. I don't profess to be an expert." The alpha studied the rug on the floor between them.

"Are you trying to warn me away?"

Koren's gaze lifted, reestablishing the vital lifeline. "Possibly. I've enjoyed being single for a long, long time. I work all hours of the day and night—whenever an idea strikes me—and I've never been beholden to or responsible for anyone. I'm not sure I make a good alpha."

Chay realized Koren was freaked out. He hadn't meant to come off sounding like a lunatic. He was grappling with unfamiliar feelings. Luckily Chay had been there before. He reacted the way he wished just one of his exes had reacted when Chay had come on too strong.

He took Koren's large hand between his. Immediately, the frantic energy rolling from the larger man calmed. "How about this? Let's go out to lunch. Let's eat some good food while we get to know one another. We don't have to settle the future now. It'll happen when it happens."

"I felt like you should know what you're getting yourself into."

Chay got to his feet and tugged Koren with him. "I'm getting myself into a lunch date, and so are you. Tell your inner dragon to simmer down. If he's really, really charming, I'll kiss him again after the date."

"I'm not charming," Koren growled as Chay locked the door behind them. "I'm usually a disorganized mess, and I'm usually so focused on my work that I forget the world outside my lab exists."

In the elevator, Chay favored Koren with a sweet smile. It was really nice to meet someone who didn't make him guess about whether and how much he liked him. "Tell me about this work that makes you forget the world outside your lab exists."

Koren twined his fingers with Chay's. "I'm the head of R&D for Draco International. I develop product ideas and prototypes."

"Like what? Anything I might have come across?"

"I just finished a reusable candle that we're bringing to market. Goodrich Scents developed an insert so that the wax keeps its scent after the first burning. You can burn it up to fifteen times before you have to replace it."

That sounded like something Chay's dad would enjoy. He was always burning candles around the house.

"And, you know how sometimes you need to plug something in, and the base of the charger is too big to fit into your power strip without blocking other plugs? I made one that rotates to give you more room so you can plug in anything."

"That's really useful." The more Koren talked about work, the more he relaxed.

"I'm working on a remote control mop."

Chay laughed. "My dad says that floors should be cleaned on your hands and knees, otherwise you miss a lot of dirt."

"Maybe for people with disabilities," Koren said. "I invented a whole set of dishes that make it nearly impossible to spill food or liquid. We're marketing fun colors for kids and more elegant ones to older adults who are maybe losing mobility."

The thoughtfulness and the sheer diversity of Koren's interests floored Chay.

"I made the first wireless headphones. DI owns the patent on that technology."

Chay chuckled. "You're like a jack-of-all-trades."

Koren shrugged. "I've been around long enough to have a variety of interests and skills. My kind can live up to five hundred years. I'm still relatively young." His grip on Chay's hand tightened, an acknowledgment that canine shifters had the same lifespan as a human.

They reached the restaurant, and it wasn't all that busy. The server seated them immediately and took their drink order.

Chay sat across from Koren and studied the menu.

"My friend said the bread was really good, and he also mentioned the bisque and the roasted chicken. And the steak." Now that the topic wasn't work, Koren's nerves made their return.

Chay couldn't remember the last time he'd been on a date where he wasn't the nervous one. "What's your friend's name?"

"Edgar. Um, Amar is my friend. Edgar is his omega. I haven't known him all that long, but he's my friend now too. He's a dog shifter."

Chay chuckled, and the impish part of his nature had him asking a question. "Is Edgar cute?"

Koren set his menu down. "If you're looking for my opinion, I don't have one. Edgar simply *is*. Amar thinks he's attractive, which is really all that matters. They've gone through a lot to be together, and recently Edgar gave birth to three babies. Edgar was the one who suggested I bring you to Petrichor."

Pieces began to fall into place for Chay. Koren had watched his friend fall in love with a dog shifter and start a family. Meeting Chay so soon afterward make Koren think his life was destined to follow the same path.

Chay glanced around. It was a darker space, more like a bar than a restaurant. He closed the menu as the server brought the soda and water he'd requested.

"Are you ready to order?" the woman asked.

Chay nodded at Koren, indicating that he'd made his selection.

"Steak sandwich," Koren said. "Rare."

The server asked about sides before turning to Chay. "Chicken Ceasar wrap, and can I get a side salad instead of fries?"

When the server left, Chay rubbed his hands together. "I love vegetables. Back home, my dad always keeps cut up veggies in the fridge for us."

"Us? How many in your family?" Koren folded his hands on the table.

"I have two sisters and a brother who are older, and Basil is my twin. Well, he's my littermate. Dog shifters rarely have single births. My dad and my father have been together for thirty-nine years. My siblings and I are planning a huge forty-year celebration next spring."

"Big family."

Chay shrugged. "Dogs, right? What about dragons? Do you have large litters?"

"No. Dragon births are rare. The fact that Amar and Edgar have three is unprecedented, and they're mixed breed, so nobody is sure how much each baby is dragon or dog. I'm not sure how long it'll be before they shift for the first time."

"Because they're mixed?"

"That, and Edgar is an orphan. He doesn't know much about himself or being a shifter." Koren's strong fingers slid through the condensation on his glass, a potent display of the sensual side of his nature. "Dragons don't shift until puberty."

Chay thought back over all the dogs he'd known. "Dogs shift for the first time around the six-month mark. I don't know many hybrids, though, so I don't know what's going to happen with them. But I can talk to Edgar if you want. He might like to know another dog shifter."

Koren's intense gaze brightened. "He'd like that. He's really friendly. People tend to like him immediately. I'll set up something."

"Invite him to Lizz's party on Saturday."

"Sure. Tell me about you, Chayton Sadler the Fifth. How long are you in town?"

"Six months." For some reason, he didn't tell Koren about the terms of the will. "I inherited the apartment, but I'm not sure I want to live there long-term."

"Perhaps you'll meet a handsome neighbor who will sweep you off your feet."

An instinct warned him to be cautious. The server returned, saving him from having to respond. She set down plates heaping with food, and then she took off.

"So, what do you do, Chay?"

"Do? You mean, like for a job?"

"Yes."

21

Chay had to give up his job when he'd moved to Verdance. "Back home, I was a bartender." He looked around Petrichor, wondering for a fleeting moment if they were in need of a bartender. "I'm still looking for a job in Verdance."

His ultimate dream was a silly one. He wanted to be a house husband. He wanted to create a loving home environment and devote himself to his spouse and children, just like his dad had done. It was hard work, but people tended to think men who wanted those things were lazy and worthless. Society wasn't much kinder to women about that issue, but they were more understanding.

"Are you locked into bartending?" Koren licked sauce from his fingers. "I could put in a good word for you at Draco. Check the job postings on our website, see if anything there appeals to you."

Transfixed by the way Koren's tongue slid against his thumb, it took Chay a moment to respond. "Sure. Maybe. I don't have the first clue what to do in an office, though. I'm more suited to food service. I took a few culinary classes in college."

He'd attended part time for a few years, and while he'd enjoyed many classes, he hadn't found anything that called to him.

"We have a restaurant in the building." Koren's eyes lit. "Maybe you can cook for me sometime?"

"Yeah. Sure." That could be very romantic, and Chay wasn't sure he was ready to commit that much.

The conversation sped through topics, and when they left the restaurant, Koren held his hand as they walked back to their building. At Chay's door, he laid another powerful, drugging kiss on the omega.

"Invite me in?" Koren suggested.

"Not this time." Chay pulled back regretfully. "Look, I like you, but I'm not the kind of guy who rushes into a physical relationship." Not to mention he'd promised Bas he wouldn't rush into an emotional attachment.

With the tip of his finger, Koren traced the shell of Chay's ear. The strange caress sent tingles through Chay's body. "I understand. How about dinner?"

Breathing easier because his refusal had been accepted, Chay smiled. "Okay. When?"

"Eight tonight."

Two dates in one day was rushing things. Laughing, Chay said, "How about tomorrow?"

Koren held Chay's hand while he kept up a steady stream of small touches on Chay's face and neck. "I have to leave tomorrow afternoon for a business trip."

"I kind of thought you said you had a business trip because you didn't want to come to Lizz's party."

Koren pulled Chay closer for a brief press of lips. "When I don't want to go to a party, I decline the invitation. I've been around long enough to not care about providing a reason for a refusal."

Absorbing that for a moment, Chay nodded. "Sunday, then."

Koren didn't hide the battle he waged with insisting on earlier contact. Pressing his lips together, he nodded. "Sunday. We'll make a day of it."

"I'm looking forward to it. Let me know if I need to bring anything."

Koren reached around Chay, but instead of pulling him into his arms, he extracted Chay's phone from his back pocket. Without asking, he programmed his number into the contacts and sent himself a text. "I'll be in touch."

Then he brushed his lips over Chay's, a teasing kiss full of promises.

Chapter 4—Koren

"He's a canine shifter?" Ezekiel Lowry sat back in the luxurious seat on the private plane and let loose with a dorky guffaw, which was out of character for him. As Head of Security for Draco International's headquarters in Verdance, Zeke wasn't at all awkward. He was a formidable dragon shifter. In his human form, he dwarfed just about everyone, and he was supermodel handsome. He looked like a picture of a buff hunk after it had been airbrushed and retouched.

Koren rubbed his palm along his thigh. Telling Amar about Chay had been different. Amar understood. Before he'd met Chay, even Koren hadn't truly understood what it was like to be struck stupid for someone he barely knew. When they'd joined Amar to rescue Edgar from Tito, they'd done it on the strength of the friendship.

"Yeah. He's a Labrador retriever."

"I had a golden Lab years ago," Zeke said. "Smart, loyal, and they like to play. They require a lot of time and attention, or they get depressed. I used to take mine on business trips with me because she hated being alone for long stretches of time."

Koren stared at Zeke. "He's a shifter, not a pet."

Zeke grinned. "Ask Amar how much Edgar in human form is like a Tibetan Terrier in temperament and personality."

If he was being honest, Koren liked the idea of having a mate who was smart, loyal, and playful. He loved the idea of being the most important person in Chay's life.

With a light punch to his arm, Zeke brought Koren out of his thoughts. "Tell me about him."

"I met him by accident. He lives in my building, and his mail was being delivered to my address. The moment I saw him, my dragon started rumbling and purring. He let out some kind of subsonic whine that I felt more than heard. So I asked him out." Koren thought about the way Chay's lips had felt against his. "He's young, only twenty-four. I feel like I'm robbing the cradle."

"Dog shifters live about one-fifth as long as dragon shifters." Zeke's eyes widened. "Oh, fuck. I'm sorry. I just meant that, if you're looking at where you are in your lifespan, you're not much older."

It also meant Chay would pass him up before long, and Koren would spend the majority of his years mourning his soul mate. Even with the stark evidence of those statistics, Koren wasn't deterred. "I've never felt like this about a man before. It's not something I can control."

"It's primal," Zeke said. "Dragons are primal creatures. We evolve slower than most species, and for the most part, we've hung onto our wild side."

The scientist in Koren wondered aloud. "Dog shifters represent the ultimate in a highly evolved shifter species. They've adapted to living in a human-dominated world, hiding in plain sight. Humans are drawn to dogs, so it makes sense they'd prize those qualities in a mate. Perhaps dragons are being drawn to dog shifters for the same reason—it's time for our species to evolve."

Zeke scoffed. "Apex predators keep other species in line. Dragons serve a vital function in this world. We own most business enterprises, which means we control the world."

"I'm not sure I agree that dragons are apex predators anymore. We're in hiding. There was a time when we were out in the open. Whole villages worshipped and feared us."

"They still worship and fear us, but now they don't know it's us they're worshipping or fearing. I'd argue we've evolved just fine." Zeke stood, stretching his legs and arching his back. "Though I'd buy that we need a correction. Omegas have become exceedingly rare among our kind. Perhaps dog shifters have the opposite problem?"

Koren had no idea. He'd spent one afternoon with Chay, and none of that had come up. His analytic mind considered Edgar, the only other dog shifter he knew. Because he'd been orphaned at an early age and abandoned by his pack, Edgar knew less than nothing about his origins. The more he thought about Zeke's supposition, the more it made sense. "You do realize that your 'course correction' further explains my theory?"

Huffing, Zeke went to the bar and poured himself a drink. "I'm wondering if you shouldn't bring up the fact you're dating a dog shifter?"

Affronted, Koren spat, "You're my friend. Excuse me for thinking my love life was a safe topic for discussion."

"That's not what I meant." Zeke sighed and returned to his seat. He set a glass with two fingers of whiskey in front of Koren. "I haven't been entirely truthful with you about the reason for this trip."

As the head of Research and Development, Koren had his hands in many disparate pots. Right now, Draco International was positioning itself to lead the next wave of digital security technology. They shadow-funded many startups, ensuring themselves access to the brightest minds and endless amounts of cash.

The stated purpose of their trip was to tap emerging talent markets in South America. A pit formed in Koren's stomach as he studied the amber liquid. "Why don't you enlighten me, then?"

"The High Council of Dragon Elders has put Kaysar on trial. Since I'm head of security, and I was the one holding him, I've been trying to keep you all out of it—especially Granger."

Koren stiffened. Tito Kaysar had kidnapped Edgar, and he'd planned to experiment on his babies. "I thought you were holding him at a black site?"

Zeke shook his head. "I did, for a while. But with someone as high-ranking as Tito Kaysar—he was the head of DI for over fifty years—that was a temporary solution. While I gathered evidence of his wrongdoings, I held him. Then I had to remand him for trial, which is happening right now. I'll be testifying tomorrow, and I brought you to corroborate my story. I was hoping to avoid telling Amar anything until I know if there's anything to tell. I'm hoping to put him away with my testimony, but that's not guaranteed."

Not understanding why his friend felt the need to prevaricate, Koren bought a moment to think by sipping the exquisite Bourbon. Finally, he pursed his lips. "Why wouldn't you just tell me the truth?"

Zeke shrugged. "I was hoping to drop you at the convention and not tell you anything, but I got an email this morning telling me the trial seems to be favoring Kaysar. As you were talking about you and Chay, I was weighing whether it would be helpful to have you on the stand to give insight into these mixed relationships—or if it would damage our case more to draw attention to it. Most dragons are against mixing with other shifter species. They feel it dilutes our lineage."

The arguments about this weren't very old, but they'd been part of the community for as long as Koren had been alive. It had been over three decades since the last generation of dragons had been born, and to his knowledge, Amar had the only mixed breed offspring in existence.

"Fuck," Koren said. "I don't want to get involved with this. It's politics. I'm a scientist."

"You're a dragon lusting after a canine, and you're not the first. I'm not even sure you're in the first dozen. In my research, I've come across a smattering of dragons across the globe who are mating with domesticated shifter breeds like dogs, cats, and horses." Zeke closed his eyes. "You bring a unique perspective, and I hadn't put it all together until you started talking about it from an evolutionary perspective. You have a good theory."

"It's a hypothesis," Koren automatically corrected. "An untested idea based on observation, prior knowledge, and experience."

"Whatever it is, I'm trying to figure out if it would help keep Tito behind bars or not."

Koren had no idea, and the pair spent the remainder of the flight in quiet contemplation.

The High Council of Dragon Elders had been headquartered in Montevideo. Though many of the members had homes in the mountains, they also kept a sizable compound in the city. Koren had never been to Uruguay before, and on the ride from the airport to the apartment in the building owned by Draco International, he found the mix of old world and new architecture to be breathtaking.

Summer in the States meant winter in South America, but the weather in Montevideo was pleasantly cool, more like a fall day than the bitter cold of a Rocky Mountain winter.

Koren emerged from the cab and stretched his legs as he surveyed his surroundings. The Draco International building housed corporate offices on several floors, and the upper floors were reserved for shifter apartments.

Looking up at the tall building, Koren imagined spreading his wings and jumping from a balcony on one of the upper floors. He could glide straight out over the water, his belly blending with the night sky. It was one of the things he loved about living on the fourteenth floor, though sometimes even that didn't seem high enough.

He inhaled deeply, taking in the scents that made up this place. Mixed in with the wet cement and car exhaust were the spicy aromas of local foods and the heavy saltiness of oceanic waters.

Zeke handed Koren his bag, and the pair checked in with security at the front desk, where they were given a keycard to access a small apartment on the twelfth floor. "When's the trial?"

"Tomorrow morning." A tall man with dark hair and eyes came toward them. He wore a fine suit with greenish undertones. His olive skin glowed in the bright glow of lobby lights. He extended a hand. "Zane Velan. I'm heading up arguments against the accused."

Zeke smiled. "Ezekiel Lowry. We spoke on the phone."

"Yes." Zane turned a friendly, professional smile toward Koren. "And you must be Koren Tafari?"

"That's me," Koren confirmed. "Are you here to prep us for the witness stand?"

27

Zane chuckled. "Among other things. Let's head up to your apartment. We have a lot of ground to cover before tomorrow."

They'd spent the day in an airplane. Koren wanted to get out and stretch his wings, but he followed Zane and Zeke into the elevator instead.

The apartment was small, with two closet-sized bedrooms linked by a small room with a sofa and a kitchenette. At least the bathroom featured a wide shower stall to accommodate the height and breadth of a typical dragon.

Zane brought a chair from one of the bedrooms and spread some papers on the coffee table. "Okay, let's talk about the proceedings thus far. It's a hearing, not a trial. The most important thing to understand is that Dragon Laws and Customs apply. We're used to human laws and customs, so that's one of the most jarring differences for your average shifter."

With a sigh, Zeke raked his hand through his hair. "You're saying there's a good chance Tito will be exonerated?"

Zane shrugged. "The High Council is comprised of older-generation dragons, and so far, they've been sympathetic to Kaysar's arguments. He's a traditional dragon. He speaks well, and he has a reputation for furthering Sharp-Winged interests. Even if they don't agree with his methods, they seem to be intrigued by his ideas."

Zeke motioned to Koren, who leaned against the wall next to the sofa. After sitting on a plane for so long, he was restless. "Koren had an interesting theory about dragons and dogs." Then he summed up Koren's argument for why he and Amaricio had fallen for canine omegas.

Zane steepled his hands under his chin and thought for several moments. "Dragons have always been purists. Breeding outside our species has never been an acceptable practice."

The scientist part of Koren's brain scoffed. "Even Kaysar was in favor of following that avenue of study."

Pursing his lips, Zane rejected the idea. "So, you want to argue that Tito Kaysar should be imprisoned because he had the right idea but the wrong execution?"

Zeke shrugged. "His methods were cruel and criminal."

"Cruel, yes," Zane agreed. "But it is the purpose of this trial to decide if his actions were criminal or not."

A thought struck Koren. "You're not convinced?" How could they win if the lawyer didn't believe in the premise of the argument?

"I think the exploitation and harm of other species is wrong," Zane said. "That's my strategy so far—narrating the physical and psychological harm being done to omegas of other species. It would be helpful if I could put Edgar Granger on the stand."

"Amaricio will not consent to that," Zeke said. "That's why I brought Koren. He was the one who assessed Edgar's fragile state of mind when we rescued him."

For the next several hours, Zane coached Zeke and Koren to make sure their testimony was relevant and would stand up under cross-examination.

Later that night, curled up in a bed that was slightly too short, Koren called Chay, but the omega didn't answer, so he left a message. "Hi, Chay. I know it's late, and you're probably asleep. I just wanted to say hello and let you know I'm thinking about you."

Chapter 5—Chay

The phone rang as Chay smoothed the lines on his black polo shirt. The insignia above the left breast showed the logo of Petrichor, where the *O* was in the shape of a raindrop, and a clustered trio dripped onto the *I* in lieu of the usual dot.

Chay had landed a job bartending at the very restaurant Koren had taken him the day before.

He hurried to the bedroom and scooped up his cell. "Felicity, how are you?"

His sisters and brothers called often, which made him feel less homesick. On the other end of the line, she laughed. "I'm okay, Chay. Guess what? Bette and I finally saved enough for a down payment on the twenty acres we need to open a wildlife refuge with Cole."

"Congratulations." Excitement gushed from Chay. "I'm so happy for you both. I wish I could come and help you build barns and stuff."

Since he had twenty-four weeks left on his exile, he wouldn't be able to be there for his siblings, and that struck a raw nerve in his heart. Chay firmly believed that family came first—always—and he hated not being able to go back home. But sticking out the six months meant he would be able to help his fathers, and once he had the money from the sale of Chayton the Second's swanky apartment, he'd be able to help fund food and medical care for the refuge.

"I know, Chay—I know. Please don't feel bad. I know you'd be here in a heartbeat if you could. You have to remember what you're doing is very important for our fathers. How are you doing?"

"I'm fine." He checked his hair and teeth in the bathroom mirror as he talked. "I found a bartending job, and I'm getting ready to go to work."

"That's great news," Felicity said. "I know how much you love bartending."

Bartending let him meet a wide variety of people, and serving alcohol almost always made people happy. Chay liked a happy crowd. It fed a piece of his psyche that craved positive energy. "It's my first day. I have a week of training. I have to go in early to learn the register and get the lay of the land."

Every bar stocked their alcohol differently, and knowing the location of the different ingredients was paramount to effectively serving customers.

"Call me tomorrow and let me know how it goes, okay? I love you, little brother."

"Love you too. Mwah." He made a dramatic kissing noise and ended the call.

An hour later, he found himself behind the bar in Petrichor, a place where people came for the food during the day and for the atmosphere in the evenings. A young bartender named Hoot had been entrusted with his training.

Hoot was a short man with a big personality. He was curvy about the hips, and he had a particular way of tilting his head. Together with his horn-rimmed glasses, Chay figured that Hoot's owlish appearance had given rise to the nickname.

Having tended bar for years, it didn't take long for Chay to figure things out. Petrichor served basic mixed drinks, and many patrons wanted beer. Rock music played over the speakers, but nobody danced because there wasn't a dance floor. Since it was a Thursday night, business was brisk, and time flew.

At the end of the night, Hoot showed him how to close out the register and divide up the tips. Hoot's eyes grew wide as he counted the jar. "Damn, Chay. You don't even flirt that much, and you almost doubled the amount of tips we normally get."

Chay grinned. He'd never had an issue with people disliking him. "People just like a friendly face." Over the course of the evening, a few customers had slipped their numbers to him, and he'd shoved them into his pocket even though he had no intention of calling anyone.

When he arrived home, he found a voice message from Koren. Listening to it elicited warm, fuzzy feelings.

The next morning, Chay hadn't been up for more than a minute before Lizz appeared at his door. He opened it to find her smiling face glowing with excitement. "Are you ready to plan the party?"

Chay looked down at his ratty pajama pants—once he found a comfortable pair, he hated to part with them—and scratched his bare belly. "I'm ready for breakfast."

"It's almost noon." Pushing past Chay, she came inside.

The omega in him didn't begrudge her assertive bearing. His sister, Felicity, was also the kind of woman who took over and made fun things happen for all. "I work evenings, so I don't get to bed until around four."

"Oh, sorry. I didn't know." She set her bags on the sofa, parked her hands on her hips, and looked around. "I see you haven't changed much."

Yawning, Chay said, "Wait here while I freshen up and get dressed."

In point of fact, he'd changed nothing. While it wasn't decorated to his taste, he wasn't planning to make this a permanent home. He'd sent out letters asking relatives to list the things they wanted in writing and mail the list to him—snail mail, not email—then he would begin clearing out Chayton the Second's belongings.

When he returned, he found that Lizz had kicked off her shoes and made herself comfortable on the sofa. She'd unloaded some things from her bags, and they were scattered over the coffee table.

She looked up, a smile lighting her eyes. "Nice. If I wore orange drawstring pants, I'd look like a pumpkin. You pull it off."

Chay hated when people put themselves down. He was in the habit of looking for things to like about people, and he liked Lizz's friendliness and outgoing personality. "Pumpkins are cute. That's why it's used as a term of endearment."

Her eyes widened for a fraction of a second, and then she laughed. "You are a sweetheart." She motioned him closer. "I'm thinking we keep it casual for the party. I budgeted for wine and finger foods. People are mostly going to want to pop in and say hello."

Gesturing to the surroundings, Chay added, "Take a look at the reclusive Chayton Sadler the Second's digs."

"That, too." She giggled. "Your uncle was friendly, but he only lived here a couple months out of the year, and never for two in a row."

"He liked to travel." Chay didn't understand wanderlust. He liked to explore his surroundings, but he preferred to do it near his pack. His uncle had a bit of malamute in him, and as such, he had a thirst for exploring new vistas, and he didn't care if he had a companion or not.

Lizz leaned back against the sofa and closed her eyes as if imagining the places Uncle Chayton had gone. "I'd love to travel like that—just pack a bag and go."

"I'd be lonely." Chay pursed his lips and looked over the list of foods she'd selected. His stomach growled. "If you don't mind, I'm going to get some breakfast. Want to bring this into the kitchen?"

She popped up suddenly, on her feet so quickly the canine part of him went on full alert. Scooping up her things, she threw them back into the cloth bags. "Absolutely. No problem." She picked up two of the bags, and a third fell to the floor.

Chay grabbed it. "Are you hungry? I was just going to have a bowl of cereal, but you're welcome to join me."

"Thanks, but I already had lunch. I'm on a gluten-free diet."

He didn't understand fad diets, but he kept his mouth closed because people tended to be touchy about that kind of thing. "Want some juice?"

"I'm limiting my sugar intake, so I'm avoiding fruit."

Some diets were just plain weird. "So what do you eat?"

"Meat, meat, and a side of meat."

Chay could get behind that kind of diet, but he noted an incongruity. "But most of the stuff you got for finger foods involve sugar or gluten."

"That's so I stay away from them." She sighed. "I work out and eat right, but I can't seem to lose weight."

Pouring himself a heaping bowl of granola cereal, Chay scowled. "Healthy is about how you feel, not how you look. Stop buying into the way society thinks you should look, and embrace the wonderfulness of you."

"Easy for you to say," she grumbled. "Tall, dark, fit, trim, and handsome doesn't have a lot of insight into short and round."

He knew that people could be assholes about other people's weight, but he made a raspberry sound. "You're fun to be around. If I was straight, I'd be into you."

"Yeah, all the gays say shit like that to me."

Shutting up, Chay resolved to invite his brother Cole for a visit. Not only did Cole look for personality first—most canine shifters chose partners by smell and instinct—but he also preferred his women to have full figures. "Lizz with two Z's, I'm going to help you find a man who loves and adores you the way you deserve to be loved and adored."

In response, she opened an app on her phone. "I have food and drinks covered. Have you thought about party decorations?"

"I can't say I have."

"How was your date with Koren Tafari?" She slipped in that question. It was casual at the start, but by the end a sense of wonder had taken over. "He's usually so mysterious and keeps to himself. I've never seen him interested in anything that didn't have to do with himself before."

Lizz clamped her hand over her mouth. "Holy cow—that sounded so bad, like he's self-absorbed or something. He's always been polite to me."

Chay could see where Koren was self-absorbed. On their date, he'd been singularly concerned with starting a relationship with Chay. Koren was the kind of man who was either completely interested or uninterested in people and their lives. He chuckled between bites of cereal. "He's intense, and I get the impression he works a lot."

"So, how did it go?"

Thinking back over his date, Chay couldn't stop a silly grin from stretching his lips. "It went well. We ate at Petrichor, where I'm now working as a bartender, and then he asked me out for Sunday."

Lizz sucked her top lip as she thought. "I'm trying to figure out if I know you well enough to ask if he's a good kisser."

Chay snorted. He felt comfortable with Lizz, like she was the kind of person who would be friends with him forever. "He's a fantastic kisser. I was a little wary at first because he's a little older than me, but I'm not sure that matters much. I like him."

"You know what you really need to worry about with that one? He's a dragon shifter, and dragon shifters have a ruthless side to them. Be careful."

Chay froze with his spoon lifted halfway to his mouth. He'd opened it up, and now his jaw fell, making it gape really wide. Lizz wasn't a shifter. Was she? Gathering his wits, he snapped his jaw shut. "Come again?"

"Dragon shifter." Lizz rolled her eyes. "Oh, come on, Chay—you're some kind of shifter, aren't you?"

This was a real gray area. On one hand, humans weren't supposed to know about shifters. On the other hand, Lizz seemed to have puzzled things out for herself. Was she looking for confirmation, or did she already have it? He settled for staring as if she'd sprouted horns.

"My mother's people were brought to Verdance over three-hundred years ago as caretakers to the beasts, which was what they called the dragons." Lizz pressed her palms to the table. "Really, they were slaves. But eventually the Sharp-Winged Tribe learned to care for themselves. They set our people free, and they became titans of industry. My people stuck around for the jobs. I used work for Draco as an administrative assistant, and now I'm the building manager here."

"Are you—are your mother's people shifters of some kind?"

Lizz shook her head. "Just regular humans."

"Oh. Okay."

"Chay, please don't take this the wrong way, but I know you're a shifter because there's no way Koren would have asked you out otherwise. Shifters don't date humans." She nailed him with a direct look, and for the first time, her perpetual smile was absent.

He exhaled hard. "Lizz, please don't be offended when I tell you I can't have this conversation with you."

"Yeah. Okay." She methodically repacked her bags. Chay didn't recall when she'd extracted items from them. "I'll take care of the decorations, and I'll come back around four on Saturday. Your uncle used to have a cleaning service come by to tidy up. Did you want their number?"

"No, thanks. I'm not opposed to cleaning a house." Chay pushed away his empty bowl. He didn't need to glance around the kitchen to note the areas he'd recently cleaned. The place had been dusty and musty from disuse when he'd arrived, and he'd vacuumed and dusted every surface. "You're mad at me."

"No, I'm not." She didn't look at him.

He got to his feet and went to her, taking her hands in his. "Lizz, please don't be angry."

"Then stop treating me like I'm clueless. We have lots of shifters in Verdance. You can't walk a hundred feet without seeing one. Animal control treads very lightly in this city." She faced him. "I'd just like to meet one who isn't ashamed of who he is."

Chay straightened up. "I'm not ashamed of who I am."

She snorted. "If you can be open about being gay, why can't you be open about being a shifter?"

"Because people who are fundamentally different aren't quite accepted. Maybe shifters don't want to be the subject of medical experiments or the target of mass hysteria." He ran a hand through his hair. "Could you imagine if dragon shifters were real? People would freak out."

She leaned closer as if to share a secret or utter a threat. "Dragons are real, Chay. They're dangerous in human or dragon form, but they don't go looking for trouble. I don't know what kind of shifter you are, but you'd better be careful. Nobody and nothing is as powerful, beautiful, or terrible as a dragon."

Speechless, he watched her finish gathering her things and head toward the door.

He caught her before she could leave. "Lizz, please don't leave. Give me a moment, okay? Where I'm from, humans have no idea about my kind, and we don't go around advertising our existence."

"Neither do the shifters in Verdance. I'd imagine shifters keep hidden all over the world for the reasons you stated. However, I'm not prejudiced or blind. I'm okay with people who are different."

Something about her invited confidence, so Chay took a chance. "I'm a canine shifter—a Labrador retriever."

Lizz dropped her bags and bounced up and down, flapping her hands. "I love dogs. Can I walk you?"

"I'm not a pet." Chay guessed he was going to need to explain this a lot as he met different kinds of shifters and the humans from Lizz's mother's line who knew about dragons. "And I like to run. There's no way any human on foot is going to keep up with me."

"Oh—that's where you disappear to in the mornings. You shift and go for runs."

This was more truth than he wanted to face when he'd been awake for less than a half hour. "Lizz, can we go back to talking about the way Koren kisses?"

"Okay, but first answer one question."

"One question," he agreed.

"When you're in dog form, and you stick your nose in people's crotches, is that considered a come-on?"

He slung an arm around her and steered her back to the kitchen. "Shifters don't do that. It's one way to tell a pure canine from a shifter."

Chay spent the next few hours getting to know Lizz. She told him a little about her people, and he told her a bit about his. He'd officially made his first friend in Verdance.

Chapter 6——Koren

"Good morning, Councilors." Next to the podium, Zane bowed deeply.

In front of him, arranged in a crescent, sat the seven members comprising the High Council of Dragon Elders. Each shifter had achieved at least four hundred years of age. They wore the traditional long purple robes, and those who still had it, sported tufts of white hair.

Four were alphas, and three were omegas, all men except for one female alpha. As was the custom, all served anonymously, though names could be had if one bothered to search.

"Thank you, Mr. Velan." One of the omegas spoke for the rest. "I see you have brought new witnesses to testify?"

"Yes, Councilor."

The omega lifted his chin. "Begin."

Zane motioned for Zeke to sit in the lone chair next to the podium. "Ezekiel Lowry, Head of Security at Draco International."

Zeke squeezed Koren's shoulder as he rose from his seat in the gallery and navigated the steps down to the small stage. The hearing chamber was set up like an indoor amphitheater, with all the action happening in one corner of the room.

In the front of the gallery, Tito Kaysar sat with the three advisers assigned to help him navigate the proceedings. The imposing dragon had been a mentor to many Sharp-Winged dragons for the past three hundred years. Though he was still strong and vital, the salt-and-pepper of his hair and the deep lines in his face testified to his advancing age. Tito was closing in on his fourth century, and he hung onto his air of power with an admirable tenacity.

As his friend took the stand, Tito Kaysar leveled a pointed look at Koren. When Koren had been young, Tito had appeared in the remote mountain village in the Rocky Mountains where some Sharp-Winged Tribe had made their home. The villagers had heralded him as a returning hero, and Koren had been awestruck when the larger-than-life figure had taken an interest in him.

Tito was responsible for Koren's career in science and technology. He'd supported every area of interest that had struck Koren's fancy, whether or not it coincided with DI's business plan.

Thinking back over all the ways Tito had enriched his life, Koren felt a pang at the current situation. While he'd never minded debating with Tito, he hated being on the opposite side of a momentous issue. Unable to deal with the emotional anguish, Koren dropped his gaze.

Unlike court back home, being in front of the High Council had no rules except that a witness must answer every question asked.

Zane stood silently behind the podium.

The omega began. "Mr. Lowry, you are the dragon responsible for imprisoning Mr. Kaysar."

Zeke faced the questioner. "Yes, Councilor."

An alpha male shot the next question. "Why?"

"Mr. Kaysar had kidnapped the pregnant omega of another dragon. We found and freed the omega, and I held Mr. Kaysar for trial."

The members of the High Council exchanged glances. The female alpha spoke next. "It is our understanding that this omega is not a dragon shifter."

"He is not," Zeke confirmed.

"Then why is Mr. Kaysar's behavior a problem?"

"For several reasons, Councilor." Zeke rubbed his palm on his thigh, the only indication of nerves. "First, the omega had been claimed and impregnated by a dragon shifter. Second, dragons aren't the only shifters on the planet. It's in our best interest to maintain amicable relations with other shifter species, which won't happen if we condone kidnapping and experimenting on them. Third, it's just plain wrong to treat other sentient beings as if they were common beasts."

"He broke no laws." Another alpha male voiced that truth.

"Customs." An omega tossed out the single word.

The alpha claiming no laws had been broken scowled. "Councilor, please speak in complete thoughts."

The omega grinned. "He broke with customs. Dragons have never hunted other shifters. We've always left them alone. In turn, they work for us when we need work done that is suited to their species." He lifted his hands, indicating their location. "This entire building was constructed by shifters. Our servants are shifters. There isn't a law governing our interactions, but we have millennia of customs between us."

The female alpha frowned. "Customs aren't law."

"No," the last alpha male agreed. "However, it is a consideration. I am more interested in Mr. Lowry's first argument. The canine shifter

38

was impregnated by a dragon shifter. Does that afford him any protections under our laws?"

A second omega spoke up. "In the past, it has not. The Sharp-Winged Tribe does not recognize half breeds. It never has."

At this, Koren inhaled deeply. Chay was back home right now, and though their relationship was just beginning, Koren already had plans to raise a family with the canine shifter. The proceedings directly impacted the way his future family would be treated by his brethren.

Zeke cleared his throat. "With all due respect, Councilors, perhaps that's where we're getting it wrong. Omega dragons have become increasingly rare, especially in the last two hundred years. Many of our kind have no idea what it was like when omegas were as plentiful as alphas. The High Council itself has more omegas on it than I've met in my lifetime."

The last omega nodded. "This is an unfortunate truth, but I don't see what it has to do with your imprisonment of Tito Kaysar."

Koren wished he could see Zeke's face. He recognized his friend's resolve when he sat up straighter and squared his shoulders. "Councilor, in my opinion, Mr. Kaysar stepped over the line when he imprisoned a shifter. Even if the High Council doesn't share that opinion, I think it should recognize that Mr. Vidal's offspring are part of the dragon community. As such, they should not have been the subject of experimentation by Mr. Kaysar."

The alpha female stared for a moment, and then she said, "Thank you for appearing today, Mr. Lowry. You're excused."

An alpha male motioned to Zane. "You have another witness."

Zane glanced back at Koren. "His testimony would be the same."

"We'll hear it regardless." The alpha male insisted.

Without waiting for Zane to motion him forward, Koren made his way to the witness chair. Once he was seated, Zane made the introduction. "Koren Tafari, Head of Research and Development for Draco International."

"Mr. Tafari," the alpha male continued. "Do you agree with Mr. Lowry's testimony?"

"Mostly, Councilor."

He rubbed his hands together sedately and leaned forward. "Where is your area of disagreement?"

"I feel Mr. Lowry—and Mr. Kaysar, for that matter—don't adequately understand the connection between a dragon and his mate. It's understandable because they've never experienced it. Until a few days ago, I had not either."

At this, Tito leaned forward, his dark eyes glittering with anticipation.

Emboldened by the momentous feelings he had for Chay, Koren elaborated. "Dragons have little choice in their mates. Once you encounter the person you're meant to be with, your dragon takes over. It craves the taste and smell of your mate. It yearns for his touch and the sound of his voice. It purrs. It growls. It insists. Denying it means damaging your dragon in the worst possible way."

One of the alpha males scowled. "This isn't relevant testimony."

"Bear with me," Koren asked.

"Councilors," Zane interjected. "Mr. Tafari is an inventor and scientist. Like a laboratory, the ingredients of his thoughts are scattered. I would argue that he will eventually come to a point not much different from the ones Mr. Lowry made."

Koren didn't appreciate being called disorganized and rambling. He understood his point, and he did not struggle to communicate it. "Councilors, which among you is or has been mated?"

"Questions of us are disallowed," an omega cautioned. "Please make your point."

"In the past two generations, virtually no omegas have been born. What if that's by design, Councilors? What if we've done it to ourselves by insisting dragons only mate with other dragons? Of the species that comingle, they're thriving. We're going extinct." Koren looked at each Councilor in turn, imploring them to see other shifters as equal to dragons. "Extending our protections to them would be mutually beneficial."

That same alpha male wore his scowl more eloquently than words. "None of this is relevant."

"My intended mate is also a canine shifter." Koren pointed his gaze at Tito. "I want to know that my mate and my offspring will be protected as I am."

After Koren spoke, Tito replaced Zane at the podium. Always an alpha among alphas, he swept his gaze across the members of the High Council, ensnaring them in his thrall. "Councilors, perhaps I breached custom when I took Edgar Vidal for purposes of studying him. As Mr. Tafari indicated, our species is dying out. The fact that Mr. Vidal was able to conceive at all was a miracle, and in studying that miracle, I hoped to understand the science behind it. Would the offspring be dragon, canine, or hybrid? Could we use canines as surrogates to overcome the problems posed by the lack of omegas? All five species of dragons are facing this catastrophe. These are questions that need answers, and I merely sought to find them. My goal was the preservation of dragonkind. It always has been. Thank you."

Tito strutted back to his seat, and Koren understood why. The proceedings had greatly favored him.

The High Council excused the witnesses and observers in the gallery so they could deliberate.

Outside the chamber, an older dragon approached. Like Koren, he had broad shoulders and intense blue eyes. Unlike Koren, his grooming was immaculate. Koren grinned and opened his arms. "Dad, I didn't know you'd be here."

"And I didn't know you'd met your mate."

The pair embraced warmly. "Is Father here?"

"No. He couldn't make it, but I wanted to support Tito. He's done so much for our family." Yeah, Koren heard the admonishment in his dad's voice.

Ignoring it for now, Koren turned to Zeke. "Dad, I'd like to introduce you to one of my best friends, Ezekiel Lowry. Zeke, this is my dad, Wyllin."

"Zeke, I've heard a lot about you." Wyllin shook Zeke's hand.

"I hope he left out all the bad stuff," Zeke grinned. "It's great to meet you, Wyllin. We were about to get lunch. Did you want to join us?"

"Sure," Wyllin said. "From your testimony, I understand why you two did what you did, but I'm not sure it was the best course of action. Tito Kaysar is a good man, and he's always worked to make life better for Sharp-Winged Dragons—specifically the two of you. Anyway, I want to hear all about this intended mate you've found, Koren. Is he really a dog shifter?"

Koren exhaled hard at the mixture of censure and wonder in his dad's voice. While his parent didn't approve, he seemed like he was endeavoring to understand before settling on a judgment.

Wyllin had been in Montevideo for a few days, so he used his experience to lead them to a nearby restaurant and order the daily special for each of them. Though Koren and Zeke were alphas and Wyllin was an omega, they knew better than to contradict a parent.

He folded his hands and faced Koren. "Okay, son. Help me to understand this trend toward canines that seems to be going on with you and your friends."

Scoffing, Koren drew his brows together. "Dad, it's not like that. It's not like we're making a conscious choice. The moment I met Chay, my dragon went crazy. It wanted him in a way I've never experienced with another man. I barely know him—we had lunch together once—but he's all my dragon is focused on. Right now, it wants me to get on a plane and fly back to Verdance."

Sitting back, Wyllin stared at his hands and thought. After several long moments had passed, he sighed. "That's what it was like for your father. Omegas are cautious by nature. While we feel an immediate connection, we require coaxing." Wyllin lifted his gaze, nailing Koren with a stern look. "I would not choose this path for you, my son. No dragon will recognize such a union, and your offspring will be ostracized."

The stark truth of his dad's warning hit Koren squarely in the stomach. He'd avoided thinking about the consequences of sating his dragon's demands because he knew he had at least one friend who would understand and accept. He returned Wyllin's steady gaze. "What about you and Father?"

Wyllin shrugged. "I cannot speak for your father, but for myself— my heart is torn. I want to say I understand, but I don't. I can promise you my love and support. Tell me about this Chay person. Do you have a picture?"

Koren hadn't snapped one yet. "No. I'll send one when I get back. He's a Labrador retriever. Right now, he lives in the apartment below me, but he doesn't plan to make it a permanent residence. He has a large family that lives on the other side of the mountains, and he plans to return there in about six months."

"Unless you convince him to stay." Zeke grinned and chucked Koren on the shoulder. "Plenty of time to work your magic."

"Magic?" Koren puffed out his chest. "Skill, you mean."

Wyllin rolled his eyes. "It's not a game. Be yourself, Koren. You're a good man."

The next morning, they all trudged to the top floor to hear the High Council's verdict. When the crowd settled down, Tito stood before them. The podium had been removed, making it clear a decision was being handed down.

The alpha male who'd insisted Koren's testimony was irrelevant spoke. "This case has brought up questions concerning the gray area between law and custom. Tito Kaysar, your actions have shed light on issues that concern every dragon in the Five Tribes—that of the extinction of our species. Omegas have become rare, and that is dangerous. You sought to study the problem in hopes of finding a solution—a commendable endeavor. However, our customs prohibit kidnapping shifters from any species, and we have updated our laws to reflect that. From this point forward, it is against our sacred laws to imprison or hold shifters of any species, and any experiments conducted must be done so with the informed consent of each participant. We would encourage you and others to continue to study on the matter, as it seems we cannot stop younger dragons from mating with non-dragon shifters. The status of non-dragon mates or any offspring arising from such unions is still a matter open to debate."

At this point, he paused to sip from a glass of water. Those in the gallery tittered, waiting for the rest of the verdict.

"Tito Kaysar, the High Council of Dragon Elders clears you of all charges and cautions you to take the new laws into consideration when designing future studies. We reinstate you as CEO of Draco International. You are free to go."

Stunned, Koren sat still as the hearing ended and most of the shifters in the gallery swarmed around Tito to congratulate him.

Zeke squeezed Koren's shoulder. "It's not a loss. They made a law protecting non-dragon shifters. That's progress."

"My mate and children will have no standing in my world." Koren couldn't seem to move. "It's like Edgar and the babies don't exist. Amar—"

"Amar doesn't care," Zeke said. "He was quite clear we were either with him or against him. He knew full well the dragon community wasn't going to embrace Edgar. Maybe this signals the beginnings of a split with the old ways. I don't know."

Koren didn't have answers. He wanted nothing more than to get home to Chay, to take him in his arms and protect him from dangers unknown and unnamed.

"Koren?"

The familiar voice jolted Koren from the fog that had enveloped him. Automatically he rose to his feet. "Tito."

Tito held out a hand, a proffer of peace. "No hard feelings?"

The feelings weren't hard as much as they were the product of volatile uncertainty.

He met Tito's gaze, searching for signs of ruthless insincerity. The ruthlessness was there, but it was tempered by affection and authenticity. "If you go after Edgar or Chay, there will be."

Tito nodded. "I'm looking forward to getting to know them."

Zeke chuckled. "You think Amar will let you near Edgar or their children?"

"I handled the situation incorrectly," Tito admitted. "I will make amends with Amaricio. Time heals all wounds."

Now that he'd met his mate, Koren lacked Tito's confidence. Nothing would ever be the same between them. The lines of division were neatly and clearly drawn, and Tito was on the other side—with the majority of dragons.

This did not bode well.

Chapter 7—Chay

Music blasted through the speakers. Chay lowered the volume as the last group of guests lingered, and he started cleaning up cups and other trash partygoers had left scattered throughout the living room and kitchen. At least they'd stayed in the social areas and left the study, library, and bedrooms alone.

A couple of the lingerers helped with trash detail, but most of them took the hint and left. Lizz was among those who remained, and she organized Tamil, Anaya, and Fareeda by assigning them areas.

"They're the rest of the advisory and welcoming committee," she'd explained before the party began. Tamil and Anaya occupied apartment 1A. They'd been married for over thirty years, and their grown children were scattered around the country. Fareeda lived in 6B with her elderly parents. She'd moved home after college to take care of them while launching her career as a high-powered attorney or a struggling Legal Aid lawyer—she hadn't yet chosen an identity.

Fareeda and Lizz were both friendly, and Chay found himself grateful that one or the other stayed by his side throughout the night. They'd smoothly introduced people, and they'd kept him circulating through the room.

Chay had been amazed by how many people had come.

"Thanks for putting this together and for helping with the cleanup," Chay said. "I think we had a great turnout."

"Agreed." Fareeda yawned. "Chay, I hate to be a party pooper, but I'm exhausted. Do you mind if we come back in the morning to help you finish cleaning?"

Meeting people excited Chay, so he was still riding an energy wave. It was going to take some time for him to come down, and he knew he settled down best when left alone. "That's not necessary. There's not much left to do."

He saw them to the door, and then he changed the music to one of those stations that played sappy music late at night and had a DJ with a sultry voice. Then he set to work wiping down surfaces and mopping the floor.

An hour later, he felt good about the cleanliness level, so he changed into pajama pants and washed his face. As he debated the merits of having one more glass of wine, a knock sounded at the door. He hadn't come across anything left behind that might indicate the return of a guest, so he peered through the peephole, curious about whom he might find.

Koren waited on the other side. His gaze was pointed toward the elevator, perhaps because he was rethinking the lateness of the hour. He ran a hand through his messy hair, and he struggled against exhaustion to hold his shoulders high. The strap of his travel bag was slung over his shoulder. He'd come straight to Chay's place before going home.

Most men played it cool at the start of a relationship, checking the urge to call against whether it might come off as a desperate or overeager move. Koren seemed to have no knowledge of that playbook, or else he disregarded that time-honored custom. Basil was going to laugh his ass off when Chay told him he was the more restrained of the pair.

Chay disengaged the locks and opened the door.

Koren's gaze raked up and down Chay's body, openly admiring his bare chest and the way his pants rode low on his hips. Wordlessly, he stepped into the apartment and swept Chay into his arms. His greeting was a passionate kiss that ravaged Chay's senses and made his inner canine whimper for more.

His hands, strong and knowing, roamed Chay's back. Gradually they slid upward until they were buried in his hair. Koren cupped Chay's head, a loving and dominant gesture, and he controlled the kiss.

After a long, long time, Koren sealed his forehead to Chay's. Their chests heaved as they caught their breath.

"Hello," Chay said as the gentle flute of a love song played a sweet melody in the background. "Did you have a good trip?"

"No." Koren closed his eyes as if shutting out painful memories.

Chay's heart went out to the mysterious man who made him feel strange and momentous things. "Want to talk about it?"

Abruptly, Koren released him and stepped back. He ran a hand through his hair, but it had a negligible impact on the sensual disarray. His gaze darted around the apartment, but he didn't appear to see anything. "I want to taste you."

Then his intense, predatory gaze locked onto Chay.

Koren licked his lips. "I need to taste you."

Though they hadn't taken that step in their relationship, Chay knew exactly what Koren wanted. What's more, he could somehow feel the alpha's need. It was a physical force, and the omega in him responded in a way Chay had never experienced before.

"You can say no." Koren's massive body was one long line of tension, a testament to what it cost him to hold himself in check. "You can send me home, and I'll come back in a few hours for our date."

Chay didn't want to send him away, but he wasn't sure he was ready to take the next step. "I wish you would talk to me—tell me what happened to upset you so much."

Koren clenched and unclenched his fists. "I can't believe this. I can't fucking believe this. The timing sucks, but I wouldn't change it for the world."

Unsure how to respond, Chay didn't move. Behind Koren, the door was still open, an escape route for either of them. Though Koren was larger and infinitely more dangerous than any man he'd met, and he seemed to be so upset that anything might make him snap, Chay didn't feel threatened.

Moments passed.

Chay went around Koren to close the door, but Koren's hand closed over his, stopping him. "I'm sorry. I shouldn't have come here. I'm in no condition to be around others."

Turning his hand, Chay caught Koren's in his, and then he nudged the door closed with his foot. He faced Koren without releasing his hold. With his free hand, he drew a fingertip along Koren's jaw. "So talk to me. Tell me what's bothering you. You came here for a reason."

Koren's gaze roamed Chay's face with the gentle force of an unexpected caress. "I came here because I wanted to suck your cock. I need to taste you. I don't know why, Chay. I don't understand it myself. I only know that my dragon demands it."

"Why?"

Blinking, Koren broke the spell he'd been weaving through Chay's subconscious mind, unwittingly stoking his desire. "What do you mean, *why?*"

"Something set you off." There was no way Koren had spent three days in this state at a business conference.

Koren snorted. "The sight of you. Your scent. The very idea of you. My dragon wants you, Chay. It wants to claim you. It purrs when you touch me, it's anxious when you're not nearby, and it rages at the idea something might happen to you. There is no reason behind my feelings. It's primal instinct."

Chay's much more domesticated instinct told him something more was wrong. "Koren, if you're serious about me, then keeping me in the dark isn't a great way to start a relationship. I know your dragon wants me. I can feel the spirit of your animal wrapping around me. But

46

that doesn't explain why you're so upset. It doesn't tell me why you were patient and willing to let things unfold naturally when you left, and you returned with an almost frantic energy."

"Dragons don't analyze feelings. We just have them."

With a wry chuckle, Chay led Koren to the sofa. The alpha followed, frustration rumbling from his chest. Chay sat, pulling Koren down next to him. Through it all, he maintained physical contact, holding Koren's hand to keep him calm.

He tucked his leg under him and rested an elbow on the back of the sofa, and he squeezed Koren's hand reassuringly. "Okay, we know you're upset. Now we need to discover what made you this way. Did it start at your meeting?"

"Yes." Koren scowled. "I don't want to talk about it."

"Well, you're going to have to. Look, I know you probably can't tell me the science-y stuff, and that's okay. I'm not likely to follow you anyway. But you can give me the broad strokes." Chay flashed his most encouraging smile.

Silence followed as Koren studied Chay's face and peered deep into his eyes. Tension and the weight of something heavy stiffened the lines of Koren's body, and none of it eased.

"Koren, trust has to start somewhere."

Koren started. "I trust you."

Not willing to debate the issue, Chay lifted a shoulder.

"No, really—I do. It's just—a lot happened, and I don't want to scare you away."

Taking a stab in the dark, Chay said, "You told your friends about me, and they pointed out that a 118-year age difference was a huge obstacle?"

"No. You're a consenting adult. They've been supportive."

"Okay." Chay didn't know where to go next, so he opted for one last plea. "Look, I'd rather not guess. We've only been on one date, so I don't feel like I know you well enough to have a real clue. I'd prefer if you just told me."

Koren's hold on his hand eased, and he traced a finger along Chay's knuckles. "Dragons aren't open-minded about alphas who have relationships with omegas from other species. My trip was to testify at a hearing. I testified against releasing a man who kidnapped and tried to experiment on Edgar while he was pregnant. You remember I talked about him—my friend's canine omega?"

Stunned, Chay nodded. He recalled Koren mentioning the man who'd recommended the restaurant. From Koren's tone, he figured that the trial hadn't gone the way Koren wanted. "He's free now?"

"Yes."

"Even though he kidnapped someone?"

Koren withdrew his hand, and he went back to clenching his fists. "Dragon law doesn't recognize non-dragon shifters as having equal rights. Though Tito was censured for his actions and warned not to do it again, he was also praised for taking steps to preserve the Sharp-Winged Tribe and encouraged to continue his experiments."

Koren closed his eyes. A muscle ticked on his jaw, and his fists shimmered as they shifted to talons for a brief second. "He's my boss. He's the CEO of Draco International. He was my friend and mentor. Everything I have is because he believed in me and took chances on my ideas. Until he kidnapped Edgar, I looked up to him. And now he's back."

It was a lot to take in.

Instinctively Chay looked for the positives. "At least they stopped him. Edgar is free, and his babies are safe, happy, and healthy."

"They didn't stop anything." Koren nailed Chay with that intense gaze, though it held more than a hint of desperation. "We did—Zeke, Eli, Amar, and I went after him. We had to break in and free Edgar. It wasn't pretty. People got hurt. Zeke is the Head of Security at DI. He arrested Tito, and we both testified against him. And now he's free."

Seeking to calm his alpha, Chay took Koren's hands in his again. "You're afraid he's going to go after Edgar, or you're afraid you're going to lose your job?"

"Neither." Koren's scowl and the tumult inside him eased.. "He needs me. He needs all of us, and he was told to get consent for any other studies he wanted to conduct."

"You don't want to work for a boss who's a douche?"

Again Koren shrugged. "Tito has always been a jerk, and it never bothered me. For that matter, I'm not much better. If Amar hadn't been involved, I'm not sure I would have been against the studies he was conducting. Really, we need to figure out why dragons keep having alpha offspring. Without omegas, our species is dying out."

This was a side to Koren Chay hadn't anticipated. It seemed cold and hard, matching Lizz's warning about how dragons were ruthless and dangerous. Though Koren behaved like an alpha, he had been warm and approachable on their date.

"I'm tempted to use our relationship as a case study," Koren continued. The scientist part of him seemed to take over. He sat forward and rubbed his jaw as he thought. "Perhaps compare it to Amar and Edgar's to find a pattern that might point to a solution."

Maybe because the turn the conversation had taken was setting off alarm bells in Chay's mind, he blurted, "But how is giving me a blowjob going to help with any of that?"

48

Koren stopped short, like he'd forgotten the stated purpose of his visit. "What?"

"When you got here, you said you wanted—needed—to taste me. You asked to give me a blowjob. Now that I know what's wrong—you're upset circumstances are forcing you to question the way your instincts interact with your morals—I'm wondering why you thought sucking my cock was going to solve the problem." Part of Chay wondered if Koren's mentor was driving him to confront this difference or if the presence of Chay in Koren's life was the cause.

"Salve it, maybe." Koren flashed a charming grin, though his eyes remained somber. "Chay, I can't fight my dragon. Dragonkind doesn't understand or approve of what's going on between us, but my dragon doesn't care. It wants you in a way it's never wanted anyone before, and I know it'll destroy me before it lets me walk away from you. And I have no desire to fight it."

It wasn't the romantic declaration Chay had always imagined. He swallowed down the disappointment. "You're saying your dragon wants to possess me and knock me up, and you're on board with the plan even though the rest of the dragons are against it."

"I don't care about the others." Koren got to his feet and stalked around the room, changing direction when he came to the fireplace, window, or a piece of furniture. "There's more here than I imagined possible. You said you wouldn't be able to follow me if I wanted to describe an issue related to my work, but you discerned the essence of what was bothering me in a way I could never be able to do. You're smart and sensible. I like conversing with you. I like spending time with you. I even like how you made me talk to you even though I didn't know what to say. You—you helped order and clarify my thoughts and feelings. I've lived with the jumble for so long, I didn't know it could be sorted out."

"So, what do you want now?" Chay had to know.

"Same things as before, but now I know why I want them." Koren stopped in front of Chay and pulled him to his feet. "Knowing the purpose makes a difference."

"How?" He agreed knowing the purpose for something made a difference. It was why he was so willing to go along with Basil's admonition for him to not rush into anything.

"Because now I know I want to build a life with you. My alpha nature requires I possess you, but that's only the beginning of what you're going to eventually mean to me. I took you out before because I wanted to seduce you into wanting to be my omega. I came here tonight because I needed to claim you. But now I understand claiming you is not just a sexual act." Koren brushed a short lock of hair back from Chay's forehead. "You're...domesticated. Instinct doesn't guide you the way it guides me. That's a difference I'm going to have to deal with. It's a difference I need in my life, and so I'm going to make you fall in love with me, Chayton Sadler the Fifth. I'm going to make you want me the same way I want you."

Whether it was the proximity or the vehement and selfish romanticism of Koren's declaration, Chay found himself beating back a tide of desire. His omega instinct responded to this alpha's authority even as his better sense warned him against being reckless.

"So, this boss of yours? Do you think he'll come after me?"

Koren stopped short. Behind his eyes, his brain moved at a million miles per hour. Eventually he exhaled hard. "If I was in his place, I'd try to insinuate myself in your life so I was privy to any data I could get. Chay, I don't want you working for Draco International."

"That's okay." Chay grinned. He didn't want to work for a huge corporation. "I got a job bartending at Petrichor."

Chapter 8

Koren

The need to taste Chay had not diminished. Koren wanted to kiss Chay senseless, strip him naked, and suck his cock until that precious seed erupted in his mouth.

"You—you're a bartender? Seriously?"

"I'm a good bartender."

"I don't doubt it." Koren paused to gather his thoughts. His goal wasn't to communicate disapproval of Chay's choice in careers. Or, jobs. Being a bartender wasn't a career. Owing a bar might be, but... He was getting off track. "Selfishly, I was thinking it eats up your evenings, and I was hoping to claim them."

Chay grinned. "You work at all hours of the day and night, and I get the sense you travel regularly. No job I get will line up perfectly with your schedule."

Koren thought about how Amaricio kept Edgar close. "I could hire you as my personal assistant."

Laughter burst from Chay, who threw his head back and clutched a hand over his heart. "No, thank you."

The offer had been rashly made, and Koren remembered he didn't want Chay working for DI. Even if he hired Chay outside of DI's reach, the job would bring him too close to Tito on a regular basis. Koren sighed. "You drive a hard bargain, and patience is not my strong suit. At least kiss me before I go."

"That, I can do." Chay stood on tiptoe and let his head fall back as Koren wrapped his arms around the sexy omega's waist.

Koren brushed his lips lightly over Chay's, the gentle buss conveying a wealth of affection. For the first time in his life, kissing a man wasn't a merely a means to a sexual end. Chay moaned softly as he moved his hands up Koren's chest and tilted his head to deepen the kiss.

Running his thumb along the line of Chay's jaw, Koren captured his lips in a kiss that seared a permanent brand on Koren's soul. Though he kept it from going too far—Chay had made it clear he wasn't ready for more—it was by far the most sensual experience of Koren's life.

This was what had been missing.

This was why wars were fought.

This was what made life worth living.

Reluctantly he put space between them. "Sleep tight, Chay. I'll see you in a few hours. Wear comfortable jeans, and bring a jacket."

Exhausted and strangely sated by a mere kiss, Koren slept solidly. He woke to Amar's ring tone on his cell. With an ancient love song in his heart, Koren grabbed the phone. "Hey, Grange. How are you?"

"Seriously? The man who terrorized my omega and tried to kidnap my children is out of prison and returning to Draco International, and you're wondering how I am?" The displeasure in Amar's growl came through the line clearly.

Having voiced similar concerns to Chay, Koren understood why Amar was upset. "Don't do anything stupid, Grange."

"Like what? Kill him?"

"The High Council was very clear that it supported his mission, just not the way he carried it out." Koren went into the bathroom and ran a brush through his hair. "If you kill him, they will come after you."

"You found an omega who isn't a dragon shifter," Amar said. "I can't believe you're blithely accepting his return."

The opposite was true. "Keep your friends close and your enemies closer." On the plane, Koren had decided the High Council wasn't completely in the wrong. "Amar, don't quit. Don't threaten Tito. I know you don't want to, but work with him. You don't have to socialize with him or invite him to your place for dinner, but I think it would be a huge mistake to not monitor his activities."

On the other end, Amar made a strangled sound. "You want to know what the worst part of all this is?"

"Not knowing the exact nature of the danger facing your omega?" It was impossible to combat a problem that couldn't be identified.

"No. It's knowing that the High Council wasn't wrong. The last generation of dragons is over forty years old, and there were only a handful of us born."

Being part of that last generation, Amaricio had grown up without playmates or siblings. Koren's generation had been three times as large, though it was still small. Koren exhaled. "They didn't extend our laws and protections to our non-dragon omegas. That worries me, especially when I think about all the older dragons who cling to tradition and a notion of a pure race."

"It makes me want to take my family somewhere and hide them from dragonkind," Amar admitted. "My kids aren't yet old enough to shift. I'm not holding out hope they're more dragon than dog. It doesn't matter much to me—I love them no matter what—but others won't be so accepting."

"Oh—Chay says canine pups shift at about six months. Since dragons don't shift until puberty—and I'm guessing dragon DNA is dominant over canine—it's likely you won't know anything for years to come. But you never know."

A moment of silence marked Amar processing new information.

"You can't hide," Koren said. "You'll spend the rest of your life looking over your shoulder."

"Tito is calling a meeting for tomorrow morning," Amar said. "I'll hear him out, and then I'm going to warn him to stay away from Edgar and our children. Can I count on you for support?"

"For fuck's sake, Grange—you don't have to ask. Of course you can count on me. Even if we weren't in similar situations, you can count on me. You can count on all of us. We had your back then, and nothing's changed now." Koren glanced at the time. "Look, I don't mean to cut you short, but I'm meeting Chay in a half hour, and I just got up."

Amar snorted. "Edgar said to tell you to wear the tangerine shirt."

Edgar's advice had been solid so far. "I will. I'll call you tonight."

"That's only necessary if the date doesn't go well," Amar teased.

Given the way Chay was slow-walking their courtship, Koren knew he was sleeping alone that night. In the background, Koren heard a chorus of babies, and for the first time, a yearning echoed inside him.

A half hour later, he led Chay through the kitchen of the omega's apartment and to the balcony.

"How do you know where everything is?" Chay asked. "You said you hadn't been inside when my uncle lived here."

"My place has the same floor plan." Koren opened up the black backpack he'd brought with him.

"What's in there?"

"Lunch." He extracted a device composed primarily of straps. "And a saddle."

"A saddle?"

Koren held up the contraption. "I'm going to fly us to a secluded place for a picnic lunch. You're going to ride on my back. We're going to try out a saddle I've been working on for the last few weeks, but I'm going to need you to put it on me after I shift."

After handing over the backpack and harness, Koren kicked off his shoes and removed his shirt.

Holding the items, Chay watched Koren and chewed his lower lip. "Why are you undressing?"

"You keep your clothes on when you shift?"

"Sometimes."

Koren knew what Chay wasn't saying—that he wasn't ready to see Koren in the buff. "I shift into a much larger creature. Anything I'm wearing when I shift gets shredded. You may turn around. I'll tell you when it's safe to look." With a sly grin, he couldn't resist adding, "Your choice, of course. If you want to watch me undress, I'm okay with that."

Though Chay didn't turn his whole body, he averted his gaze. With a shimmer of light, Koren shifted into a Sharp-Winged Dragon. His dragon form was significantly longer and thicker than his human form.

Okay, it's safe.

Chay's eyes widened, and his head whipped to face Koren. "Did you just talk to me inside my head?"

Yes. This is how I communicate while in dragon form. Does it bother you?

Chay's gaze moved over Koren's body, taking in his dark scales, lethal talons, and long body. "Can you hear what I'm thinking?"

Koren had been prepared for the question. People, in general, didn't want others intruding on their thoughts. While he was good at reading facial expressions and body language, those skills came from decades of practice, not any special endowment that was a result of his dragon side. *No, but I have excellent hearing. When we're flying, and the wind is whistling in your ears, you can speak normally, and I'll hear you.*

"How do you talk to other dragons?"

We communicate through telepathy, mostly in images, ideas and feelings. When I speak to a non-dragon, I must formulate and project words.

Chay considered this. "That's a really cool super power. I only have enhanced hearing and sense of smell."

How do you talk to other dog shifters?

With a rakish grin, Chay let out a deep *woof.*

Koren rolled his great dragon eyes, though he knew the lizardlike slits only appeared to be looking up briefly. Those sorts of expressions were far less effective in dragon form.

Still, Chay caught the gesture, and he laughed. Then he held up the saddle Koren had fashioned. "You're sure you want me to saddle you up and ride you?"

The tone Chay used hinted at a multi-faceted meaning behind the question. Koren quite enjoyed the flirting. *I guarantee it'll be the best ride of your life.*

With a chuckle, Chay lifted the saddle onto Koren's back, positioning it higher than his wings. Koren appreciated that Chay either had common sense or good instincts when it came to this. He talked Chay through attaching and adjusting the straps. It didn't take too long, and for the first time, Koren cursed the fact that he couldn't really feel Chay's light touches on his scales as he smoothed the straps.

"Koren, not to be a killjoy or anything, but thicker straps would make for a better design."

He assured Chay. *They're secure.*

"It's not that," Chay added. "They look like they're going to dig into your scales, maybe even slide underneath to irritate you. Is this the first time you've tried it on?"

Yes. Dragons are surprisingly reluctant to use technology that might domesticate us. I made this in secret, at home, after Amar flew Edgar over the Andes without anything for him to hold onto. It was a very dangerous trip. Recalling the strange maneuvering in which Amaricio had engaged to keep Edgar from plummeting to his death had inspired Koren to create a dragon saddle.

It was basic, but it had a place to sit, stirrups for the feet, and a place to hold on. There was even a belt to secure the rider. It did not include any mechanism that might allow a rider to steer. That would be beyond the pale.

"So this is your first official test flight?"

Yes.

"Do you have a travel plan in the event this doesn't work out?"

No. It'll work.

"I like a confident man."

Smart. Koren drew his dragon brows together as he corrected Chay. While he might be confident in general, his invention exemplified his intelligence. *I studied hundreds of designs already in use, and I adapted them to fit my needs.*

"Nerds are sexy." Chay put his foot in the stirrup, chuckling as he climbed aboard. "I'm going to ride a nerdy dragon. That's something I never imagined saying." Once he was in place, a consideration occurred to him. "Aren't you afraid people will see you?"

My underside blends with the sky, and the human brain has a remarkable capacity for ignoring facts right in front of their faces.

Koren flew Chay out of the city and into the mountains. He landed in a secluded meadow inaccessible to anyone who lacked wings. A stand of evergreens surrounded it, the verdant green needles stretching high to compete for sunlight. That left plenty of room at ground level for shade-loving shrubs to provide undergrowth that would hide smaller creatures. At their arrival, three brown bunnies hopped to safety.

Chay climbed down, and Koren shifted. Without the massive body under it, the saddle dropped to the ground at Koren's feet. "Well? What did you think?"

A sly grin curved the corners of Chay's very kissable lips. "I think you're extremely well hung."

Koren resisted the urge to glance down. He held out a hand for the backpack containing his clothes and their lunch. "I'll get dressed so you're not tempted to jump me."

Unzipping the pack, Chay extracted the clothes Koren had worn to his apartment. He handed them over, his gaze never wavering from Koren's. "I didn't mean to give you the impression I wasn't tempted to jump you, Koren. I find you very attractive, but I don't want to make the mistake of rushing into a relationship. We might yet find out we're not at all compatible."

"We're compatible," Koren scoffed as he shimmied into his jeans. Though it was summer, the high altitude meant there was a chill in the air. "How about you spread the blanket and set out the food? I skipped breakfast, so I'm starving."

Unbidden, the desire that had driven him to Chay's apartment the moment he arrived from Montevideo returned. The delicious aroma of the lunch he'd packed tempted him, but Chay's scent called to his basest desires.

Swallowing back the need raging in his veins, he knelt on the blanket and helped Chay unpack the food.

Chay

Wind swished through the treetops, and the strong odor of pine failed to wash away the pheromones emanating from Koren. Sharing a blanket with the sexy, mature man was an exercise in restraint.

Last night, Koren's scent had been inviting, but today it was almost irresistible. In ten short hours, it had strengthened, and Chay's sensitive canine nose could focus on nothing else. He scooted to the edge of the blanket and stared into the trees, willing the odor of white pine to overpower the temptation.

When Koren had shifted to human form, he'd looked around the meadow with his sharp, predator's eyes. Completely unaware of his physical beauty or the way it affected Chay, he'd ensured the safety of their location before leisurely dressing. Chay witnessed all of this in a state of heightened awareness, uncannily in tune with the Koren.

Whether he was ready to admit it or not, his canine had accepted the dragon as his alpha. Now Chay needed to deal with the conflict between his instincts and his rational brain.

Never in Chay's life had the urge to jump on an alpha and offer himself—beg, plead, whatever it took—been so overwhelming. Keeping his promise to Basil was strenuously taxing his willpower. He thought about Koren's kiss, the way the alpha's lips had felt on his, the way he'd held Chay in his arms, and a tremor of anticipation ran through his body.

"You don't have to eat it if you don't like it."

"What?" Jerked from his brooding thoughts, Chay found his gaze drawn directly to Koren's bright blue eyes.

"The sandwich. Not everyone likes turkey. It's okay. I brought salad and breadsticks as well, and brownies for dessert."

Chay didn't care one way or another for turkey. The vegetable fixings and the dressing on the sandwich provided the flavor anyway. "The sandwich is fine."

Wariness crept into Koren's eyes. "You don't like the setting?"

"The setting is idyllic." He gazed at Koren meaningfully. "Very romantic."

The wariness left, chased out by triumph. "That's what I was going for."

"You bring a lot of your dates here?"

"No." Koren set his half-eaten sandwich on a napkin. "You're special, Chay. I thought I was very clear about that fact."

"Crystal," Chay agreed. But he still knew very little about the man whose presence made him want to strip naked and offer his submission. "How many serious relationships have you had?"

Koren had been around for almost fifteen decades. Chay expected that he'd engaged in a few long-term relationships. Though Chay had only been dating for ten years, he'd been in two serious relationships, and he'd attempted a dozen more—which was why Basil urged him toward caution.

"Including this one?" Koren picked up his food and took a huge bite.

"Yeah." Chay had never been with a man whose mind was as resolute as Koren's.

Koren finished chewing, and then he chased it with a long pull of water, likely buying time as he counted his past boyfriends. Finally he nodded. "One."

"One?" The weight of what was going on between them settled on Chay's shoulders. "Really? In over a hundred years, you've never taken a lover or anything?"

"Taken a lover?" Koren chuckled, and amusement sparkled in his eyes. "I haven't heard that phrase in years. Yes, I've had lovers. I've even kept some of them around for several years. However, those were distractions, not relationships. Like I am with you, I've always been open and honest about what I want or don't want. My lovers knew our dalliances were just for fun."

Existing like that sounded so cold and lonely. Chay's heart went out to Koren and to all his former lovers. Everybody deserved to be loved.

"Hey." Koren slid his hand along Chay's lower back until it curled around his opposite side. Then he pulled Chay into a loose embrace. "You're looking really sad right now. Tell me what you're thinking."

Koren's enticing scent was so much closer now, and Chay couldn't resist turning his face into Koren's neck and inhaling. It calmed his nerves, but it quickened his core. "I was thinking your life sounds really lonely."

Koren's hand smoothed a caress up Chay's spine, and his fingers teased in the short hair at the nape. "I have friends and family, so I've never been lonely."

"Being with someone you love is different."

"I know." Koren's voice was suddenly thick with desire and meaning. "You've been in love before?"

"Yeah." Chay was honest by nature. He didn't see the need to hide his past from Koren. "A couple times. Bas, that's my brother, says I fall in love at the drop of a hat."

"That seems a bit melodramatic."

"He's not wrong," Chay admitted. "That's why I'm so insistent we take it slow. Usually I rush into a relationship, and then a month later, I'm a heartbroken mess."

Koren pressed a kiss to Chay's temple, and his fingertips skated over the sensitive skin below Chay's ear, sending erotic signals to all points. "You're saying you're intent on making us take our time because you want this to work out?"

Chay wasn't sure about anything. Koren was from the city, and Chay didn't want to live in the city. Koren was a dragon, and while that seemed cool, recent events brought a bit of terror into the idea. Then there was the age difference to consider.

Despite all that, Chay wanted nothing more than to close his eyes and let nature take its course.

Rather than respond, Chay threw out another question. Urging caution and getting Koren to talk had worked the night before. "Have you ever had your heart broken?"

"No. And I won't break your heart, Chay. I can swear to that." Koren's lips slanted over Chay's, brushing softly and promising so much. "I've never rushed into anything. I'm cautious by nature, studying every angle before making a move. Rest assured I know this is the real thing."

The part of Chay that was loyal to Bas and wanted to protest seemed to vanish as Koren's kiss took on an urgency that lit a fire in Chay's blood. With a moan, he twisted so his chest was against Koren's. The heat of contact made his head spin, and then the alpha's tongue swept into his mouth, claiming his will and eliciting a soft groan.

Instinct took over, and Chay found himself straddling Koren's muscular thighs. Koren wrapped his arms around Chay, holding him close as he ravaged Chay's lips with an endless kiss.

Chay pushed until Koren was on his back, and in the new position, he ground his cock against the bulge in Koren's jeans. Like a wild man, he tore at Koren's clothes. His efforts proved ineffectual, and Koren didn't seem to notice he was thwarting Chay's attempt to disrobe him. He kissed Chay with unrestrained passion, his hands roaming Chay's back and cradling his head.

Before Chay knew what had happened, he found their positions reversed. Koren's larger body covered his, pinning it to the ground. Soft blades of grass pillowed his backside through the blanket as Koren's strong, knowing hands explored his chest and arms. Drugged by kisses, Chay surrendered to the bliss. Feelings he'd never imagined suffused his very being, and instinct took over.

When Koren lifted his shirt and kissed a path up his stomach, Chay only gripped the alpha's head, urging him with subsonic moans and whimpers. Koren's tongue flicked over his nipples, teasing them to a peak, and then he latched on, sucking and biting the small nubs. Beneath him, Chay writhed and arched.

"Like that, Chay?" Koren's breathy question penetrated the fog of need clouding his brain.

"Yes." Needing to be closer to the sensual aroma wafting from Koren, Chay buried his face in the alpha's neck. "You feel so good, Koren."

"I want to taste you," he said. "But I'll stop if you think this is moving too fast."

It seemed as if he'd known Koren his whole life, at least on some level, and at his instinctual core, he knew he belonged to the dragon shifter. The promise he'd made to Basil faded in the face of these momentous feelings, but it didn't completely erase.

"Taste me," Chay said. "Please."

Koren grinned as he kissed his way back down Chay's body, and his chest rumbled with a purring sound. "You're so fucking handsome, Chayton Sadler the Fifth. I could spend hours kissing and touching this magnificent body—and one day, when you're ready, I will."

Unzipping Chay's jeans, Koren lifted the canine shifter as he slid the denim down his legs. Koren nipped at the sensitive skin on Chay's thighs. "So sexy."

The chill in the sudden gust of wind made gooseflesh pop out on Chay's exposed skin, and he shivered from the cold.

"Sorry, honey. It's cold up here. Let me fix it." Koren peppered kisses over his thighs, the heat of his mouth juxtaposing with the cool breeze to create a curiously erotic sensation.

Chay lifted up and slid his briefs out of the way.

Koren wasted no time. His tongue darted out to lick the purplish crown. Then he wrapped one hand around the base and closed his lips over the cock's head.

Pleasure, in the form of air, hissed from between Chay's teeth. He propped his hand under his head to better watch his cock disappear into Koren's luscious mouth. The alpha worked his shaft, wetting it and taking it deeper with each thrust. Before long, the entire length disappeared into his lover's hot mouth.

An expression of pure rapture overtook Koren's features. The rumbling purr vibrated against Chay's cock, eliciting an involuntary moan.

"Koren, that feels so unbelievably good."

Something tongue-like wrapped around Chay's cock, sucking and squeezing to an undulating rhythm. A loud moan ripped from the depths of Chay's throat. Koren gripped Chay's sac in his massive hand and gently pulled on it. The motion sent white-hot pleasure coursing through Chay's body, and he came in a sudden, throbbing burst of bliss.

Koren moaned and sucked harder, slurping up every drop of ejaculate. Then he slowly released Chay's balls and cock. He sat back on his heels and raked his gaze over Chay's exposed body.

Though Koren was still clothed, Chay allowed his eyes to feast on the sight of the man who'd rocked his world. Koren's eyes were black, his irises glowing green slits like lightning in the darkness. He seemed somehow larger, as if his shoulders were even broader and his muscles had been pumped up. The prodigious bulge in his jeans even seemed bigger.

And yet, Koren also seemed sated.

Another cool breeze blew across Chay's skin, and he pulled his pants back up. "That was amazing, Koren."

"Yes," Koren agreed with a sibilant hiss. The tip of his tongue flicked out, showing that it was long and forked. "My dragon agrees."

With that, he lifted Chay onto his lap and kissed him deeply. "I understand you want to take this slowly. I can wait to claim you, honey, because once I do, you'll be mine for the rest of our lives."

Entwined in each other's arms, they finished lunch.

"Shift for me?" Koren packed their trash and leftovers into the backpack. He glanced up at Chay, who was untangling the straps to Koren's harness invention.

"You want me to shift? Why?"

"Because I want to see you. I want to know that part of you." Koren set the pack at Chay's feet, and then he took the dragon saddle from him. "I know you like to shift at night and go for a run." He gestured to the secluded surroundings. "This is a perfect place for you to be yourself."

"Okay. Sure."

As Koren had done, he shed his clothes, and then he shifted into his Labrador form. Some colors muted, but his vision sharpened. He looked up at Koren, and he found his alpha smiling.

"You're a damned cute dog, Chay. Can I rub your belly?"

By way of response, Chay barked and broke into a run. Shifting always gave him energy, and he was in the mood to burn it off. The ground rumbled, and he glanced over to find Koren next to him, wings tucked against his long, strong dragon body. Pure glee suffused his limbs, and he headed into the woods.

The pair ran, frolicking through the forest until they came to a stream. Chay dipped his head to drink from the icy meltwater from the glacier upstream. Koren did the same. Chay noted their differences—Koren was ten times his size and a mythical beast—but he also saw their similarities. They were both black creatures with luminous green eyes, and they both loved being in their shifted form.

Thinking about Koren's request, Chay rolled onto his back, exposing his belly.

Koren's talon scratched lightly against his tender skin, honoring the trust Chay had placed in him.

With a thought, Chay shifted into his human form. "If you were talking to me, I couldn't hear you."

Koren shifted as well, and the two of them faced each other. Chay checked out his handsome, nude, future lover, and he held himself still while Koren did the same.

After a few moments, Koren responded. "I didn't say anything. One of the things I like about shifting is just being and not talking. Besides, actions speak louder than words."

A slow smile curved Chay's lips. "I like you, Koren Tafari."

Koren jerked Chay to him, and his lips closed over the omega's.

Chapter 9

Koren

Though the date had been wildly successful, Koren was home by eight. After kissing Chay senseless at his door, Koren went home and called Amar, just as he'd promised to do.

Edgar picked up the phone. "Koren, please tell me you're calling to say you can't talk long because your boy toy is in the shower waiting for you?"

Koren chuckled. "Hi, Edgar. How are you?"

"Don't change the subject. Is he in the shower?"

An image of Chay in the shower, touching his cock as he pictured Koren watching, made Koren groan. "Our date ended ten minutes ago. He's at home."

"One floor below you."

"Edgar, we're taking it slow, just like you and Grange did. We're getting to know each other."

On the other side, Edgar groaned. "We didn't go slow on purpose. We went slow because Amar didn't think fooling around with his assistant was a good way to treat an employee. You don't have that issue."

Edgar had a point, but Koren wasn't holding back because he wanted to. "Chay wants to be courted, and I'm going to make sure he gets what he wants. We had fun, and I'm seeing him again on Tuesday."

"Why not tomorrow?" Edgar pressed.

"I have to work tomorrow morning, and he has to work in the evening." Koren fully expected to show up at Chay's place the second he returned home. If nothing else, they could make out. "Edgar, I called to talk to Granger. Is he available?"

Though he only heard Edgar's sigh, he had no trouble picturing Edgar's long-suffering rolling of the eyes. "He's right here, and for the record—he agrees with me."

Amar's voice came on the line next. "Hey, Koren. How are you?"

"Your omega is very opinionated."

Laughing, Amar agreed. "He's a staunch romantic."

So, it seemed, was Chay. For the first time in his life, Koren was looking forward to romancing a man in order to win his heart. But that wasn't why he'd called. "Tomorrow, we'll listen to Tito, and then we'll take steps to make sure our interests are protected."

They spent the next couple hours discussing how to counter Tito's likely response to the new restrictions on his behavior.

The next morning, Koren sat through a general meeting welcoming Tito back from his "sabbatical." Most of the beings that worked at DI were not shifters, and Zeke had covered for Tito's absence by saying that he'd taken personal leave. The woman introducing Tito hailed him as a great leader, and Draco International employees cheered when he took the stage.

Sitting in the rear of the auditorium with Amar on one side, Zeke on the other, and Eli on the opposite side of Amar, Koren breathed to control his conflicted emotions as Tito talked about the importance of family and how DI was like one huge family. All-in-all, it was the kind of speech that left listeners feeling good about themselves and the state of the world even though nothing substantive had been communicated. The foursome retired to Zeke's office in the basement as soon as the gathering concluded.

Tito was lost in a sea of people who wanted his time and attention, but Koren knew he'd make his way down there as soon as he could peel himself away.

"He shouldn't be here," Amar thundered. "Not after the things he did to me and mine."

"He's prohibited from doing anything without consent," Zeke said. "Edgar and your pups are protected."

The pair of them went back and forth, making essentially the same points Amar had brought up to Koren the night before.

Eli and Koren sat back, watching their friends. Both Zeke and Amar were young, the last of the current generation. With their long lifespans, dragons didn't rush into having offspring, and so Amar was one of the youngest parents Koren had encountered. Though they were about a hundred years older, Eli and Koren were still considered young.

When Amar fell into a silent brooding, Eli sat forward. "Amar, you'll tell him Edgar and your family are off limits, and we'll back you up. End of story."

Blood suffused Amar's face, darkening it dangerously. "You know he won't give up until he gets what he wants. Tito is relentless."

"So are we," Eli admonished. "But I know you're going to worry anyway. We're a united front, and Tito is on his way here, so put that forbidding expression back on your face, and let us do the talking."

The door opened, and Tito came inside. Though he was just as large as the rest of them, Tito seemed bigger. Perhaps it was due to the nearly mythic positions he'd held in the hearts and minds of all the people present. His air of authority had not diminished, and it overshadowed even the air of danger emanating from Amar.

"It seemed superfluous to knock," Tito explained. "Since you're all waiting here for me."

He closed the door behind him, and he took the seat directly across from Amar at the conference table dominating Zeke's office. Amar scowled, but he said nothing.

"Amaricio, I owe you an apology. I did not truly understand the relationship you had with the young Mr. Vidal, and I let my quest to stop dragonkind from dying out interfere with our friendship. I hope one day you can forgive me." Tito flashed a tight smile. "I'm under no illusion you're feeling generous toward me, and that's okay for now."

Amar's glare didn't waver.

Tito turned to Eli next. "Ezekiel did an excellent job of communicating your concerns to the High Council and to me. I don't blame you for choosing to stand by Amar in his hour of need. Good friends are hard to find, and I admire that you stuck with yours when they needed you."

Shades of shock crossed Eli's features.

Tito faced Zeke next. "You and I have talked at length, and I intend to abide by the terms of my release. I know you'll be watching me carefully."

"Damned straight." Zeke's handsome visage remained stoic.

Next, Tito faced Koren. "As I don't blame Eli, I also don't blame you. In fact, I'm putting you in charge of researching the preservation of dragonkind."

Koren started. While he was the head of Research and Development, he was more of an inventor and less of a researcher. "Tito, I'm not a geneticist."

"Then you'd better get going on your studies. Draco International will, of course, pay for any classes you need to take." Tito got to his feet, his gaze sweeping across the foursome. "You all still work for me, and the High Council is especially interested in the results of the study. Amaricio, be sure to set aside funds for Koren's research. Eli, keep his actions from becoming common knowledge among the humans on staff. Ezekiel, you'll do what needs to be done to protect Draco International's interests."

With that pronouncement, he left.

Tense silence whizzed around Zeke's office for many moments.

Finally, Zeke chuckled. "Bastard always finds a way to get what he wants."

"So now the future of dragonkind is on my shoulders." Koren shook his head. "I'm a physicist. I hate biology."

"My family is off-limits," Amar said. "Even for you."

With a sinking feeling, Koren realized something. "He did this to drive a wedge between us."

Amar's scowl deepened. "We won't let it."

Eli sighed. "Either Tito is going to get what he wants, or he'll destroy Koren's career. That's the choice he's forcing us to make."

Koren squeezed his eyes shut and pinched the bridge of his nose. "Let me research. Let me see what I can dig up."

"I hate to say this." Zeke glanced at Amar, an apology written in his features. "But I'll have the records from Edgar's imprisonment sent to you. They're full of medical test results."

Koren shook his head. "Let's keep those sealed for now. Let me see what I can do on my own."

Amar left the room without a word.

Chay

"Bette, he's dreamy." Chay couldn't resist gushing to the one sister who fell in love as quickly as he did. "He took me into the mountains, and we had a picnic in a secluded glen. Then we shifted and frolicked all over the place."

A snort came from the other end of the call. Bette couldn't contain her giggles. "Is 'frolicked' a new term for sex?"

"No, it is *not.*" Chay's promise to Basil was on the verge of becoming a real sacrifice. "I promised Basil and Felicity I wouldn't rush into anything, and Koren has been amazing about honoring my wishes. He kisses me like the whole point of sex involves only our lips. And when I was ready to throw caution to the wind, tear off his clothes, and have my way with him, he changed up what we were doing. We frolicked, Bette. It was wonderful."

Bette sighed. Chay pictured her at the home she shared with Felicity, sitting on her sofa while the Sadler family dogs snuggled on either side of her. They probably had their heads in her lap, and they were staring up at her with their trusting and loving gaze. On the table in front of her was probably a travel magazine. She and Felicity had been planning a trip to Greece for years.

"He sounds wonderful, Chay. Maybe Basil was wrong to make you promise not to dive in. Maybe I'm not exactly objective here, but the way you talk about him—I can tell you're in love. Real love—different from the puppy love from before. Koren seems perfect for you, and I've never heard you sound so happy before. You're fulfilled."

While he agreed, so many factors were still uncertain. Yes, he had momentous feelings for Koren, but they also had a number of differences to overcome. And Chay didn't know how Koren felt about Chay's desire to be a house-husband. He confided all of this to Bette.

In the end, she said, "Chay, you need to follow your heart. Maybe you'll get it broken, but love is worth the risk."

Bette's certainty gave Chay pause. "Bette, it sounds like you've fallen in love."

"I have." She exhaled a pleased sigh. "Oh, Chay—she's wonderful. I've never met anyone like Annette. She's a golden Lab shifter, and she's definitely The One. You feel it differently than a general crush. I think about her all the time, and my canine whines when I see her. We've only known each other for four days, but I know it's the real thing."

Chay knew exactly what Bette felt. "Yeah. It's like that."

"So don't wait," she said. "If he's committed, and you're committed, then start having those conversations about what a life together will look like."

This was the advice Chay had wanted all along, and now that he had it, a burden lifted from his shoulders. He didn't feel the need to maintain distance between him and Koren. His canine howled with glee. "We have a date tonight," he said. "I'll talk to him. And, Bette? Don't say anything to anyone else."

He felt a little bad about keeping this from Basil, but his littermate would remind Chay of the promise he'd made, and Bas would hold him to it.

"I won't," Bette promised. "And you don't say anything about Annette. I'm waiting until we move in together next month to announce our engagement."

Chay spent an extra long time preparing for his date. He shaved and manscaped. He obsessed over his outfit. What jeans made his butt look sexiest? Which shirt best brought out the chocolate of his eyes? Short sleeves or long? V-neck, or a shirt where he could leave the top three buttons undone? Which aftershave would Koren prefer?

The time for their date came and went. Chay waited a half hour, and then he texted Koren.

No response.

After their last date, Koren hadn't been very communicative. He'd texted once Sunday night and once more Monday morning, but he'd been silent since then. Chay had chalked it up to their opposite work schedules, but now he was growing worried. There was no way Koren had lost interest, not with what they felt for each other, so that meant something else had happened.

What if he'd been injured? Chay didn't know his friends or family, so it was likely nobody would inform him if Koren had been in an accident.

Before he flipped out completely, Chay went upstairs to Koren's apartment. He hadn't been there before. As he entered the hallway separating the two apartments on the fifteenth floor, he noted that, except for a potted plant and a pair of leather chairs in the hall, it was identical to Chay's floor.

"This building loves cream-colored walls," he noted.

Standing in front of Koren's door, Chay experienced a moment of trepidation. What if Koren's feelings *had* changed? Maybe he'd reevaluated the idea of getting involved with a shifter from another species? Basil had been accepting so far, but maybe that was because Chay had promised not to rush into anything. Perhaps his family was waiting him out, convinced the candle of his love would sputter and burn out, and then they wouldn't have to deal with having a dragon in the family.

Chay pushed out all those unkind thoughts and the insecurity that fueled them, and he knocked on the door.

A minute passed, and he knocked again.

Another minute passed.

Worried, Chay pressed his ear to the door and concentrated. Dimly he heard music playing. Someone was inside.

He knocked again, pounding on the door this time. If Koren didn't answer, he'd go downstairs and get Lizz. She either had keys, or she knew where to get them. Either way, he was getting inside Koren's apartment to make sure his soul mate was okay.

The third effort bore fruit. The door swung open suddenly, and Koren appeared on the other side. His hair stuck up in all directions, and his bloodshot eyes had a frantic quality to them. The clothes he wore were wrinkled, and he had a streak of spilled coffee staining the front of his shirt. None of it diminished his attractiveness.

He blinked as if he wasn't sure whether he was awake or dreaming.

"Koren? What's wrong?"

Confusion marred the blue intensity of his gaze. "What do you mean?"

Chay let his gaze wander over Koren again, noting the lines of tension and the faint worry lines around his mouth. "You look like you haven't slept in days."

Frowning, Koren ran a hand through his hair, disheveling it even further. Then his frown dissolved and his eyes widened. "It's Tuesday, isn't it?"

A sense of relief swept through Chay. Koren had lost track of time. Chay flashed an indulgent smile. "Have you been working for two days straight?"

"Looks like it." Koren scratched his belly and looked over his shoulder. "I'm sorry, but I'm going to have to cancel. I'm not ready, and it's doubtful I'll be good company tonight."

As Koren had done when he'd come to Chay's place, Chay pushed past Koren and into the apartment. The layout was identical to his, but where Uncle Chayton had filled his apartment with furniture, Koren had opted for a minimalist approach. While he had the necessary basic furnishings, there was plenty of wide-open space perfect for him to spend time in dragon form.

He also had a huge collection of books. Attractive shelves had been built into most walls, and books burst from them. Unlike a library-for-show, these were haphazardly arranged. Some were upright. Others lay on their sides in colorful piles of paperbacks mixed with hardcovers and stacks of magazines. Even the upright ones had sideways books stacked on top of them. Every available inch was stuffed with reading material. Across the room, the outside wall had huge windows, and from the light streaming from the kitchen, Chay knew there was a slider that led to a balcony perfect for a dragon.

"Do you ever sit on your balcony and pretend to be a gargoyle?" It looked like the impulsive part of Chay's brain had temporary custody.

Koren stared, and then a slow smile spread over his face. He closed the door behind Chay. "A dragon and a gargoyle are not interchangeable. We're distant cousins, though."

Chay started. "Gargoyles are real?"

Laughing, Koren shook his head. "Most creatures are real."

"Unicorns?"

"Not that I've encountered, but there are winged-horse shifters."

Chay clapped his hands. "A Pegasus? I want to meet a Pegasus shifter."

"They're rare, and they value their privacy." A frown creased Koren's brow, and his eyes glazed over as he lost himself in thought.

"Maybe... I wonder..." He mumbled, but he didn't finish any of his sentences. "Could be worth..."

The last time he trailed off, Chay put a hand on Koren's shoulder. "How about we stay in? If you've been working for two days straight, you need to take a break. I'll make dinner, and we can hang out for a bit. Then I'll go and let you get back to work. Okay?"

Before Koren opened his mouth, Chay noted the forthcoming refusal.

"Let me rephrase," he preempted. "You're taking a break. While you're taking a shower and changing into fresh clothes, I'm going to make dinner for us, during which we can drink some wine, and you can rave over my cooking while telling me how wonderful I am."

He followed up his gentle directive with a kiss on Koren's cheek.

Koren's nostrils flared, and he inclined his head. A deep rumbling in his chest let Chay know Koren's dragon was exercising its will. Koren's refusal melted. "Okay. You're right. I need a break. How about I meet you at your place?"

"Here's fine." Chay rubbed his hands together. "I know where the kitchen is."

Koren fidgeted uncomfortably. "It's a mess."

Chay waved off the concern as he sailed toward the room in question. Like any fine bachelor pad, soiled dishes covered the counter near the sink, and they were mounded in the basin. Open boxes of cereal were scattered on various surfaces. Chay opened the refrigerator to find food staples inside. Okay, it was not a complete loss.

"You cook?" He peered over his shoulder at Koren, who'd followed him into the kitchen.

A smile cracked through Koren's concern. "I grew up before gas and electricity, so yes, I can and do cook." He ran his hand through his hair, making more of it stand up. "I'm usually better about straightening up. I didn't expect you to come over."

Rather than respond, Chay waved Koren off. "Go. Shower. Change. Maybe freshen up your sheets. Let me do my thing."

Koren paused. "Freshen up my sheets?"

Chay flashed a reckless grin. "Maybe you want to take a longer break tonight."

"Chay, you said you wanted to wait."

"Maybe I changed my mind."

Rather than the flirty brashness Chay had expected, Koren hesitated.

It occurred to Chay that perhaps Koren also wanted to wait. He rushed to assure his alpha. "We don't have to if you don't want to."

Koren's jaw set decisively. "We'll talk at dinner." Then he left to spend time administering self-care.

Chay set a pair of steaks to defrost in the microwave while he started on the dishes. He was a stickler for a sanitary workspace. At Petrichor, the manager had already noted Chay kept his station clean and neat, and he attended to spills immediately. It didn't take long for him to have the kitchen in order. As the dishwasher hummed, Chay tenderized the meat and made the breading for country fried steak.

A radio was plugged in next to the fridge. Chay found a station that played 80's music and he sang along with the string of classics as he worked.

When the steaks were sizzling on the stove under Chay's watchful eye, Koren returned. The wet tips of his hair left damp spots on the shoulders of his shirt, but the shirt was clean, and he'd shaved. Somehow he managed to seem larger and more imposing—completely alpha.

Chay's core tightened, quickening with anticipation, but he played it off with a grin he hoped came across as calm and collected. "Feel better?"

"Yes. You were right. Thank you." Koren slid his arms around Chay's waist and pulled him closer. "The whole apartment smells really good."

A light heat crept up Chay's neck. "I'm making banana bread. You had some bananas that were a lot overripe." The modern kitchen boasted a double oven, and Chay was very excited about that.

Koren buried his face in Chay's neck, making it clear which scrumptious scent he preferred. "I'm sorry I forgot about our date."

"That's okay." Chay was actually pleased to be cooking for Koren. He liked taking care of his man. "I fell for a mad scientist. This is what you were like when we met, you know—pulling all-nighters and working too much."

"I guess I need someone to take care of me since I don't do it for myself." He brushed a kiss on Chay's neck.

Chay's heart soared. "I wouldn't mind taking care of you."

Koren kissed a path down his neck, and then he dropped to his knees. "Then let me take care of you."

Before he could squeal consent, Koren had Chay's pants down to his knees. His hand encircled Chay's cock, coaxing it to life, and the black, forked tip of his tongue darted out.

Chay hissed as electric pleasure shot from the tip of his cock to his balls. "I thought there was something different about you."

"Hungry." Koren's voice had roughened, and his irises had morphed to reptilian slits. "Need you."

71

Koren closed his mouth around Chay's erection. Molten heat mixed with escalating desire, and Chay's knees weakened. He clutched at Koren's shoulders, and the alpha wrapped his arm around Chay's backside, steadying him. Chay forgot about the steak on the stove and the dessert bread in the oven as delicious tendrils of pleasure unwound in his core. Koren's head bobbed as he sucked the entire length of Chay's cock, and that unique tongue wrapped around this member, squeezing a tantalizing rhythm.

Dragons gave great head.

Soon Chay's balls drew up, and his orgasm detonated. Koren purred as he sucked harder, swallowing every drop. Then he drew back, the sated smile curving his lips matching the one on Chay's face.

"That was delicious." Koren got to his feet and rummaged through a cupboard while Chay fixed his pants. "It's like an elixir I never knew I craved, and now I can't imagine not having it every day."

Chay flipped over the steaks. His back was turned to Koren, so the alpha couldn't see the way Chay's eyebrows shot to his hairline. "You know, most alphas don't like to give blowjobs all that often."

Koren shrugged. "Seems about right. But now, my dragon demands this nourishment. I might be addicted."

Laughing with delight, Chay attended to the onion-and-mushroom sauce he'd made to smother the steak. "I'm willing to be your supplier."

"Good." Koren's reply was curiously quiet and pensive.

Chay glanced over his shoulder. "What are you thinking now?"

Koren shook his head. "Research." Then he set a glass of wine next to the stove. "Here. It's a good vintage."

"Nuh-uh. You're not changing the subject that easily." He sipped the wine and agreed with Koren about the vintage. "Research should invigorate and excite you, but you're almost melancholy. What's got you down?"

"I'd rather not talk about it just yet." Koren leaned on the counter near the stove and sipped his wine. "I want to forget work and relax. It's your job to keep me mentally present."

"Okay." Chay agreed cheerfully. He knew Koren needed a break. "Let's talk about sex. I was talking to my sister, Bette, and she agreed that waiting is overrated."

Koren exhaled hard. "Chay, please understand—I'm not pressuring you. I don't know why I crave the taste of you, but the fact that I do—and that you let me suck your cock—doesn't mean I expect more."

"I know." His gaze met Koren's. "I want more."

Running a hand through his hair produced a light rain of droplets on his shirt, and it ruffled his drying waves. "When we met, you set down a very strict boundary. While I'd love to take you into my bedroom and defile you in a hundred pleasurable ways, the alpha in me demands I honor your needs, that I put your best interests above all else. It's a strange feeling for me. I'm not used to caring like this."

Chay slid the breaded steaks into a pan and poured the sauce over them, and then he put the pan in the oven. He wiped his hands on a towel, and he threw it on the counter before plastering his body to Koren's. The alpha's arm came around him, holding him closer.

"I love that you care," Chay said. "And if I wasn't ready to take the next step, then I wouldn't be here, asking you to make love to me." He ground his pelvis against Koren's. "I can feel how much you want me."

"That is not in question." Koren set down his glass and stilled Chay's hips. Though his eyes were still bloodshot, he was more alert and present than he'd been since Chay had arrived. "I have no doubt we're fated mates and the sex will be mind-blowing. However, being a fated mate doesn't mean we automatically know or understand each other. I like you, Chay. I'm attracted to you. And you were right when you said we needed to get to know each other first. And so, I'm not going to take you into my bedroom, and I'm not going to make love to you—not yet. But I will give you this."

Koren's lips closed over Chay's in an endless kiss that lasted until the timer on the oven interrupted.

Breathless and more aroused than he'd ever been in his life, Chay's hands trembled as he removed the steak from the oven and the bread from the oven below it.

Chapter 10—Koren

Bent over to rummage through a low drawer, Chay's ass beckoned to Koren. He wanted to touch it, knead it, lay sucking kisses on it—but if he gave into that urge, then he'd be going against the first and only line Chay had drawn in the sand.

He'd given his reasons—his propensity to fall in love and get his heart broken—and Koren was determined to make sure that when Chay fell in love with him, it was the forever kind.

Because once he claimed Chay, losing his omega wasn't an option.

The feelings slamming through Koren were too powerful for him to distinguish between love, lust, and primal need.

The blowjob thing puzzled Koren. Chay was correct that alphas tended to prefer to receive head more than they gave it. Koren could count on one hand the number of times he'd sucked a cock in return for nothing, and both times were with Chay.

The taste of Chay's ejaculate lingered in his mouth, and his dragon purred as his tongue searched for any remaining flavor. Not only did it sate his dragon in a way sex never had, but it made him feel closer to Chay—more invested in his health and happiness. Perhaps the craving facilitated a bond between a dragon and his omega. It was an interesting theory, one he planned to discuss with Amar and Edgar, hopefully separately. Subjective research was more reliable when conducted in isolation. That way, responses weren't unduly influenced.

He refilled their wine glasses and helped Chay carry their plates to the dining table.

Chay sat down and cut a piece of steak. "I'd ask how you've been, but you don't want to talk about work."

The only reason he wanted to avoid the topic was because he didn't want to worry Chay. Koren smiled tightly. "Work has been demanding."

"Because your evil boss came back? Is he threatening to fire you?"

Now Koren felt like an idiot. He'd completely forgotten he'd already confided so much in Chay. With a grunt, he dug into his food.

"No. He assigned me to finish the research he started illegally and immorally."

Chay blinked. "What?"

"He wants me to find out why dragon offspring are almost all alphas—more omegas would be better suited to keeping us from becoming extinct—and why Amar's mate is a canine shifter. He knows about you, and I think he's expecting me to include us in my research." Koren scratched at his forehead, a gesture that indicated irritation and thought, not dry skin. "I'm stuck between a rock and a hard place."

"Wow." Chay finished chewing. "On one hand, you can't turn down the assignment, and on the other hand, you can't experiment on your best friend or your omega."

"I've been reading everything I can find on genetics research. This isn't my field of study, so I'm flying blind."

Chay ate as he thought. Koren's thoughts fixated on how much Amar was going to hate him if he asked for a cheek swab from his triplets.

Finally Chay cleared his throat. "What about the other tribes?"

Unsure what Chay meant, Koren tilted his head.

"You said there were five tribes of dragons, right?"

"Yeah."

"They must be having the same problem, right?"

"As far as I know." Koren couldn't think of any tribe that was thriving right now.

"It stands to reason Tito wasn't the only dragon to have this idea. DNA sequencing and genetic manipulation are pretty big in the science world right now. You should see what the others have on the topic, and then you should hire a geneticist you can trust—even if it's a human or someone from another tribe. Koren, I have no doubt you can master this discipline, but it's going to take time, and from the way you're holed up in here, I'm thinking you don't feel like you have a lot of time."

It floored him how smart and insightful Chay was, and it humbled him that this man wanted to be his omega. Plus, he was a remarkable cook.

"This is an excellent dish," Koren said. "What is it called?"

"Smothered, country-fried steak. The other things on your plate are potatoes. Dessert will be banana bread. Now stop changing the subject." Chay's chest puffed up with pride as he explained and admonished. He would make an excellent dad.

"Chay? What really made you want to change your mind about having sex with me?"

"Damn it, Koren. That is not what we were talking about."

"Humor me," he directed. "The other topic needs time to simmer before I continue with it."

"Fine." Chay sipped wine. "We'll table it for now."

"Thank you, darling, I appreciate it."

"So, it's not so much that I changed my mind as it's that I stopped fighting nature."

Nature—the inherent predilections of a person or species—was precisely the subject Koren was exploring with his genetic study. He sat up straighter. "Are fated mates common among canine shifters?"

Chay shrugged. "They're as common as not. Some people feel it from the start. Others take time to grow. My mistake was in thinking I should change. I'm not the kind of guy who takes my time. I'm the kind who decides from the start whether I'm all in or not. I have no idea if that's impulse or instinct or some kind of combination of the two."

Pushing his empty plate away, Koren folded his hands on the table. "Chay, you are fucking sexy when you talk like that."

"Yeah?" Light twinkled in Chay's dark eyes. "Should I whisper the Periodic Table like a list of dirty words? Will that get you hot and bothered?"

The *idea* of Chay doing that got him hot and bothered. Suddenly his alpha shifted from protecting Chay from heartbreak to needing to claim him. There was already no going back for Koren.

Koren smacked his lips. "Move in with me."

"I can't. I have to live in my uncle's apartment for six months, or I won't get my inheritance, and neither will the rest of my family." Chay grinned. "You can move in with me. We can both live surrounded by someone else's stuff."

The décor didn't matter, and besides, it was easy enough to change. Having Chay mattered.

Without committing to anything, Koren stood and held a hand out to his omega. Rather than take his hand, Chay leaped into Koren's arms. Their lips met in a clash Koren instantly mastered. He carried Chay to his bedroom where he set him on the bed. He hadn't changed the sheets because he honestly hadn't anticipated the night taking this turn. Without breaking the kiss, Koren settled his weight on top of Chay's smaller body.

He slid Chay's shirt up, taking his time to explore the silky feel of his lover's skin. He lifted the material out of the way and moved his kisses down Chay's chest. The omega arched and moaned, and his hands roamed Koren's arms and shoulders, tugging at the shirt Koren had hastily selected.

Koren refused to cooperate until a subsonic whine issued from Chay. Only then did he lift up enough to let Chay remove his shirt. They rolled, and Chay's questing touch delved under the waist of Koren's jeans, and his palm closed around Koren's cock.

"Oh, Koren. It's so big."

Laughing, Koren unzipped his jeans to give Chay more room. "I'm big all over, omega."

"Good thing I brought lube." Chay dug into his pocket and brought out a small bottle. "I came prepared."

Koren took the bottle and set it on his nightstand. "Let's get those pants off you."

Chay shimmied out of his jeans and briefs, and he toed off his socks. Completely naked, he lay back and waited while Koren looked him over. Chay was not a small man. He had strong shoulders and a lithe, defined physique. He was vibrant and handsome, utterly sexy.

Koren knelt up and scooted off the bed where he disrobed. Chay's gaze roamed his body, desire darkening his skin and turning his eyes to limpid pools of chocolate. Koren crooked a finger, and Chay scrambled to sit on the edge of the bed. Gripping his cock, Koren pumped his fist up and down. Then he put a hand on the back of Chay's head, urging him closer.

Chay nuzzled Koren's balls, rubbing his cheek and chin against them in erotic circles. Then he nipped at the tender skin with his lips. The sensations weren't quite rough, though they weren't exactly gentle either. It felt good, and his dragon purred its approval.

Dipping his head, Chay added his tongue to his ministrations. He licked as he nuzzled, wetting his lips and inflaming Koren's desire. By the time he licked Koren's length, the dragon shifter was barely holding on.

Giving up the sweet torment, Chay wrapped his hand around the base and took the crown of Koren's cock into his mouth. His head bobbed as he fucked his mouth on Koren's dick, and Koren watched, enthralled by the sight of his cock disappearing between his lover's lips.

He gripped Chay's head, holding it still while he fucked his cock deeper into his omega's mouth. Chay held onto Koren's thighs, digging his fingers in when he reached his limit.

Withdrawing, Koren directed Chay to lay back and lift his knees. "Touch yourself, my omega, but don't come."

Chay grinned. "You're bossy. I like it."

"You'd better." Koren drizzled lube onto his fingers and squeezed a dollop over Chay's cock to help him masturbate. "I'm not going to change."

He massaged the gel into Chay's sphincter, and the omega moaned loudly. "That feels so good." His hand moved lazily up and down his cock, spreading the lube. "Hydrogen, Helium, Lithium."

"In order?" Koren lifted a brow. "That's so hot."

Chay's grin grew, and his chest heaved with the effort it took to avoid exciting himself to the point of climax. "Beryllium, Boron, Carbon."

Koren lined his cock up with Chay's entrance.

"Nitrogen. Fuck, Koren—you have no idea what you do to me."

He slanted his lips over Chay's, capturing his omega's moans with a searing kiss. "Tell me. What do I do to you?"

"You make me feel vulnerable and safe at the same time. I need to feel you inside me. I need to know I belong to you."

"You do, Chay. You belong to me." Koren pressed forward, entering Chay slowly.

Chay's feet slammed down on the bed, and the omega's body bowed. "Don't stop. Please don't stop."

Koren concentrated, and concentric ridges appeared on his cock, a feature guaranteed to increase his omega's pleasure. This dragon shifter feature required a lot of self-control. If he stopped concentrating, the ribbed texture would smooth out.

To keep Chay still and to open him more, Koren pressed down on Chay's chest, and he hiked Chay's right leg over his shoulder. With a steady pressure, he fed his wide cock into his omega's body.

Desperate sounds of pleasure tore from the depths of Chay's throat. He stopped stroking his cock and grabbed onto Koren's arms. Half-formed words poured from Chay, and Koren pieced together entreaties for more.

He surged forward. "I'm in, my omega. I'll give you a moment to acclimate."

"No." Chay's head thrashed. "Fuck me, please. You feel so good, Koren."

Withdrawing a few inches, Koren thrust forward.

Beneath him, Chay trembled. Koren thrust again, establishing a moderate pace. Chay cried out and thrashed, and so Koren lifted them both, centering them on the bed. He held Chay in place with his weight while he thrust into Chay's tightness.

He wanted Chay to touch himself, but his omega was too far gone. He clutched at the pillows and dislodged the fitted sheet. Subsonic whines mixed with the loud moans of pleasure, and Koren's concentration slipped. The ribbing disappeared, and he fucked his cock into Chay's ass. His pace increased as his motions took on a frantic quality.

Chay's body stiffened, spilling seed across his stomach seconds before Koren's climax hit. It detonated in his balls, sending shockwaves up his spine and down his legs. In his whole life, Koren had never orgasmed like that. He collapsed onto his omega, his entire body shaking with the aftershocks.

When he was able to move again, he lifted Chay in his arms and carried him into the bathroom. He turned on the shower and let it warm before carrying his omega into the spray.

Under the steady fall of water, Chay roused. His eyes fluttered open, and he nestled his head against Koren's shoulder. "That was amazing," he whispered, his voice hoarse from shouting.

Koren kissed the top of Chay's head. "It was. And now you're mine, omega. I have claimed you."

Chay tilted his head back, and Koren sealed that claim with a masterful kiss. But already his mind was turning back toward the genetic problem he'd been tasked with solving.

Chapter 11

Chay

Being claimed as an omega wasn't what Chay thought it would be. He had visions of domestic bliss where he got up and made breakfast for Koren, ran errands during the day, and made dinner in the evenings before heading off to work. He pictured bouts of hot sex and lots of kissing, snuggling, and touching.

New love meant lots of physical contact. It meant long, meaningful looks and sly smiles. It meant quickies in the shower and languorous explorations in the bedroom.

Apparently Koren never got that memo.

He'd accepted Chay couldn't move in with him, and he had no intention of either moving in with Chay or sleeping over more than a handful of nights. Koren worked crazy hours, and Chay found himself in a cycle of dragging Koren out of his study for meals and watching helplessly as he returned after a half hour. Appealing to Koren's dragon generally bought him more time, and that meant Koren insisted on sucking Chay's cock regularly.

Chay called it Feeding the Dragon, and while he didn't mind, the act was beginning to ring hollow. He wanted the incidental touches and long looks. He wanted to talk and snuggle. Koren was falling down on his promise to court Chay.

Koren easily worked over eighty hours each week, and it exacted a toll. Koren had no energy for anything else, and his emotional state had taken a beating. He worked at a frenetic pace, and when he wasn't working, his mind was still immersed in the genetics study. His expression, even when thoughtful, had a brooding edge.

Chay knew Koren was trapped between a need to find answers and a dread this project would cost him everything he held dear. For his part, Chay felt neglected, and because his canine insisted it needed Koren, he also felt trapped.

He found himself spending a lot of time with Lizz and Fareeda. They weren't a replacement for his sisters Felicity and Bette, but they definitely filled a void. It didn't take long for them to become part of his Verdance pack.

A month after he'd moved to the city, his sisters had planned to visit. The morning before they were due to arrive, Chay found himself in Koren's apartment making breakfast. In a stunning turn of events, Koren came into the kitchen without Chay dragging him from the study. His shirt was rumpled, and he wasn't wearing pants.

Chay eyed the dark blue briefs, and then he let his gaze wander down Koren's powerful legs to his bare feet. "Good morning."

Koren padded to the fridge and extracted a carton of orange juice. Chay handed him a glass so he wouldn't drink directly from the carton. A frown creased Koren's mouth as he accepted the glass. Silently he poured juice.

"My sisters are coming tonight. They'll be here in time for dinner, and they're looking forward to meeting you." With practiced skill, he folded the omelet in the pan. Then he served it to his alpha at the small, rectangular table near the kitchen window.

Koren studied the egg on his plate, but he didn't dig into the meat-filled concoction.

"You don't like omelets now?" Chay had made sure to use ingredients he knew Koren liked—cheese, peppers, and sausage.

"I—No, I like your cooking. It's... Sorry. I was thinking about something else." He cut a square of egg and shoved it into his mouth.

"Of course you were," Chay muttered. He returned to the stove and grabbed the pan so he could wash the dishes.

Koren glanced up. "You're not going to eat?"

"I already had breakfast." He'd wolfed down leftover chicken soup after his early morning run. He started the dishwasher and wiped down the counter.

"I have to go out of town for meetings today and tomorrow." Koren rinsed his plate and set it in the sink.

Chay parked his hands on his hips. "You're doing this on purpose."

Mild surprise lifted Koren's eyebrows. "Doing what?"

"I told you two weeks ago my sisters were coming. I told you a week ago I had reservations for the four of us for dinner tonight. I just reminded you we had plans tonight. And now you're telling me you won't be there." Chay threw the dishtowel in his hand on the counter. "You know what? Nevermind. Don't come. You're officially uninvited."

He turned to leave, but Koren caught his arm. "You're upset."

Throwing a glare at Koren, he spat sarcasm. "You think?"

"I've been busy," Koren said. "And I've neglected you. I'm sorry, Chay, but I'm doing this for you—for us."

Chay exhaled hard. "I'm not sure there's an *us*. There's me, who's more like a cook and caretaker, and then there's you."

Koren stiffened. "And what am I?"

Shrugging, Chay pulled from Koren's grasp. "You're the guy who likes the idea of me, but who has no idea what to do with the actuality of me."

Spreading his hands, Koren entreated in an entirely alpha fashion. "That's not fair."

Chay was not swayed by the admonition. "No, it's not fair."

A dangerous light flared to life in Koren's eyes, and smoke exhaled from his mouth. "You can't break up with me. I claimed you."

That assertion rankled. Chay crossed his arms. "I can break up with you if I want, Koren. I'm not a possession; I'm a person. You don't own me. I can do what I want."

Koren grasped Chay's arms tightly and hauled him closer until their chests touched. "You're upset, and I'll allow that you have reason to be. I have been preoccupied with things you don't understand, but I'm doing this for you, Chay. I'm doing this so we can be together."

Utilizing every ounce of strength, Chay wedged his hands between them and pushed against Koren, but the alpha's superior strength meant he made no headway.

For his part, Koren didn't seem to notice Chay was trying to put distance between them. "I want a life with you. That's what I'm working toward."

"Theoretically, you are." Chay placated his alpha with a soft caress on his cheek. "But in real life, you're the guy who lives in the apartment above me that I cook for in exchange for oral sex."

Koren opened his mouth to deny it, but Chay interrupted.

"Tell me you didn't come after me to stop me from leaving before you could suck my cock."

The denial died. Koren pressed his lips together.

"Thought so." Chay jerked from Koren's hold and headed for the front door.

"I think it's a bonding thing." Koren was hot on his heels. "Amar said he has the same craving for Edgar."

Chay paused with his hand on the knob. "Maybe it's a bonding thing for you, but it's not for me." Chay never thought he'd see the day when he would turn down a blowjob. "You know what I liked? Those two dates we had were pretty wonderful. And then you claimed me, and it's like the honeymoon was over. You said you were going to make me fall in love with you. Well, you haven't done it yet."

That was a lie. Chay's heart broke as he put his foot down, but he knew he was destined for more pain if he didn't. Some alphas walked all over their omegas, and Chay wasn't willing to be a doormat. He wanted a partner who loved and respected him. He needed a partner who *needed* him. Koren *wanted* him. It wasn't the same thing.

Koren

The door closed behind Chay. Rooted to the spot, Koren listened as the latch clicked into place. Part of him wanted to run after Chay. Part of him was angry Chay couldn't see his point of view. And part of him was relieved Chay was gone. When he was there, it was difficult to concentrate on his work. The scent of his omega made his mind wander.

The smell of breakfast wasn't what roused him from a deep sleep. Chay's unique pheromone signature had drawn him to the kitchen. Koren had a meeting with Anshu Bray and Lajos Edison of the Ice-Breather Tribe, and he had to be on his A game in order to get the cooperation he needed from the rival tribe. Sharp-Wings and Ice-Breathers had a long history of antagonistic behavior, including random attacks and the stealing of R&D from each other.

Koren had spearheaded several raids in recent years, and he'd been the target of a few as well. Their animus went back too far to know who had started it all.

A few months ago, Tito had tried to forge an alliance with them by pairing up Anshu Bray—a rare omega dragon—with Amar. As Amar had been with Edgar at the time, that attempt hadn't gone over too well.

When Koren's mind was on Chayton, he didn't do his best work.

Instead of following his omega to soothe him and assure him that he was important, Koren got dressed and went to work.

He meant to go to his laboratory, but he found himself in Amar's office instead. Kimbra, Amar's capable admin, sat at her computer, her fingers flying over the keyboard as she listened to something through her earpiece. She was a younger woman, perhaps thirty or so, and she kept her dark hair in a neat bun. When she'd rebelled against Amar's instructions to pick up his dry cleaning or to arrange dinner parties at his home after hours, he'd hired Edgar as a personal assistant.

Though Edgar no longer worked in the office, he still saw to those personal details, and Kimbra was once again a happy employee.

She glanced up, smiling as he came through the door. "Vander, hold on a moment." Covering her earpiece, she motioned to the door. "He doesn't have any appointments this morning, and Edgar isn't here."

"Thanks." He rapped on the door as he pushed it open.

Inside, he found Amar facing three screens on his desk, his eyes squinting as he regarded the spreadsheets that made up the bulk of his reading material. He looked up, and his face brightened. "I didn't expect to see you today."

Koren had always been close to Amar, and now he found himself frequently in his buddy's office, seeking answers to questions he couldn't formulate. He sank into the chair opposite Amar. "I'm meeting with Ice-Breathers today and Rock-Shapers tomorrow."

Amar swiped at his eyes, likely clearing away the numbers clouding his mind. "They have research?"

"I don't know. Rock-Shapers never integrated into human societies." They spent the majority of time in dragon form, and they eschewed modern conveniences invented by humans. "I'm not sure they have any kind of science going on."

"No word from the Silver-Winged or the Fire-Breathers?"

As contentious as their relationship with Ice-Breathers was, they were still the closest thing they had to allies. "Nothing."

"Tito's policies for the Sharp-Winged Tribe have made many enemies among tribes that should be our brethren." A muscle in Amar's jaw ticked with acrimony. "But he has the High Council believing he's infallible. It's a cult of personality."

Six months ago, Koren had been a believer. Now he was in crisis because he could see this issue was a many-sided die. It was too complex for simple labels of 'right' or 'wrong' to apply.

"Chay is angry with me." Koren hadn't meant to confide, but then, he reasoned, why else had he come to Amar's office?

Amar's gaze went to the wide windows providing him with a spectacular view of the cityscape before returning to rest on Koren. "You're surprised?"

"His sisters are coming to Verdance for the weekend. He made reservations for all of us to go to dinner. I didn't know I'd be going on this trip until yesterday." Koren understood why Chay would be disappointed, but not why he'd be angry. "He said he wasn't in love with me."

Amar's shoulder lifted and fell with no comment.

"Grange, don't be an ass. I'm keeping Edgar and the babies out of my research. I've interviewed you, and I've taken DNA samples from

84

you, but that's all." He'd also recorded the same information about himself and a dozen other dragons at Draco International.

"You've also blown off at least ten invitations to bring Chay to dinner. Edgar is despairing that you're ashamed of him or us."

No such thing was true. The heat of anger traveled up Koren's neck. "I've been busy."

"Is that what you tell Chay when he wants to spend time with you?" Amar's dark eyes shot ice in Koren's direction. "Omegas devote themselves to their alpha, and it's an alpha's job to devote his life to his omega. You said Chay is always coming over to take care of you, but you never say what you do to take care of him."

Koren rose and clenched his fists. "I'm doing this for us, and for all dragonkind. He needs to be understanding."

Rising and facing him without clenched fists, Amar loomed over his desk. "Dragons live for a long, long time. Your research is important, but it shouldn't be what consumes you. That's Chay's role, and if you're neglecting him, then you're going to lose him. Do you think Edgar sticks around because he's my mate? No—it's not enough. It's a relationship, Koren, and from what I can tell, you spend more time whining to me than talking to him. That's not enough to make it work."

That wasn't at all what Koren had wanted to hear. He'd wanted his friend to take his side, to assure him that Chay was out of line, that his omega was behaving selfishly and petulantly. And Amar had all but accused Koren of those things.

Koren still sported a scowl when he arrived in Pleasance, Verdance's sister city. He'd flown himself, and so he landed on the rooftop of Anshu Bray's high-rise apartment building, where he could shift and change in relative privacy.

Pleasance was a smaller town, and it was home to Draco International's largest competitor, Gliding Principles. They'd started out in transportation, and they specialized in aviation.

Anshu Bray was his counterpart at GP, and he seemed like the most logical person to meet with.

Koren emerged from the maze of hedges on the rooftop to find Anshu waiting for him. Like all dragons, Anshu was tall and muscular, and in keeping with Ice-Breathers, he had long blond hair, blue eyes, and pale skin. In coloration, Ice-Breathers were opposites of Sharp-Winged Dragons.

He smiled, revealing an even row of white teeth in a way that didn't radiate welcome. "You came alone. That's brave."

Koren kept his gaze locked to Anshu's. "Is there a reason I should have brought backup?"

Anshu's shoulder lifted. "It's what you Sharp-Winged types tend to do. Safety in numbers or some such tripe."

For the sake of peace, Koren offered his hand. "Thank you for meeting with me. The open sharing of information is in the best interest of science."

Peering at Koren strangely, Anshu accepted the handshake. "We can meet in my apartment. I did tell GP that you were coming, so don't be surprised if representatives happen to stop by. Our last peace offering to the Sharp-Winged Tribe didn't quite pan out."

Koren winced. He hadn't been involved in the negotiating of that deal, but he'd definitely participated in the aftermath. "Tito Kaysar kind of sprung that on us at the wrong time."

"And he selected an alpha who already had a mate."

"Yeah. Well, he still should have asked first."

Anshu led him to an apartment with large rooms, high ceilings, and a decidedly modern flare. "Can I offer you something to drink?"

"Sure. Coffee?"

When the pleasantries had been observed and snacks served, Koren found himself reluctant to bring up the true purpose of his visit.

Anshu didn't share his reticence. "So, you're here to establish a connection with me before our leaders undertake negotiations for an arranged marriage?"

Koren started. That wasn't at all where he'd expected the conversation to head. They were inventors. It was natural they'd talk about emerging technology or projects on which they might want to collaborate. "I'm sorry, Anshu. I didn't mean to give you that impression. I have an omega."

Anshu's eyes narrowed. "Then why are you here?"

Setting his coffee mug on the low table between them, Koren spread his hands wide. "I wanted to talk to you about the endangered status of our species. I'm researching genetics, looking for reasons why omegas are almost non-existent and what we can do to reverse that trend."

Anshu's gaze slid away, and a frown pinched his chin. After a few moments, he regarded Koren somberly. "You want to talk to me, the only omega under fifty years old in existence, about why there aren't more omegas?"

Even among female dragons, there were only alphas.

Though he felt he'd stepped onto a minefield, Koren nodded.

"Why don't you ask me how many dates I've been on in the last ten years?"

This was awkward. "I don't see how that's relevant."

"No?" Anshu threw his head back and an ironic giggle bubbled out. "Darling, if the only omega on the planet who is single can't get a date, then you have your answer. No Ice-Breather wants to date me. Not one. When Tito Kaysar came around with his proposal to mate an Ice-Breather with a Sharp-Winged, they laughed at him. They actually behaved like I was some kind of precious jewel that had to be preserved for the right mate, only none of them wanted to be my mate. I was in the room, and when I stood up and said I would do it, all hell broke loose."

This wasn't a conversation Koren had been interested in having with Tito, and now he found himself horrified and intrigued. "I don't understand. You're handsome and intelligent. Are Ice-Breathers blind?"

Anshu shrugged. "I've never had sex. I've never even been kissed. Did you know that? Not one of my tribe is interested in even fooling around with me."

"I really don't know what to say." In the absence of omegas in the Sharp-Winged Tribe, Koren had fooled around with submissive humans and omegas from other species. He'd even fucked a few alphas.

Ruddy fury suffusing his features, Anshu shot to his feet. "I thought you were coming to offer yourself in the place of Amaricio Granger."

Moving slowly, Koren went to Anshu. He set his hands on the omega's shoulders. "Anshu, have you ever thought that maybe you deserve more than an arranged marriage? Maybe you deserve to find someone who will love and appreciate you for yourself, and not because you're a rare omega."

As he spoke, the real cause of Chay's upset finally penetrated. His omega deserved to come first. Amar had said it, but Koren, in his infinite capacity for obstinacy, had rejected his friend's reasoning. He'd even dismissed Chay's own words.

Fuck.

His omega needed him, and he'd been derelict in their relationship.

Lips grazing his jolted Koren from his thoughts. Reflexively he stepped back. "Anshu, I told you I have an omega."

"Not a dragon." Anshu didn't appear at all contrite. "So he doesn't count."

But he did. This was the prejudice Amar had faced, and it was to be Koren's lot as well. Squaring his shoulders, Koren drew his brows together in an expression of severe disapproval. "He counts. Look, Anshu, I came here because I wanted to know if you've done any research. I've done some, and I thought we'd get farther if we shared resources."

Plopping down in a huff, Anshu heaved a dramatic sigh. "I've done some gene sequencing."

Koren returned to his chair. Having a table between them made him feel a little better. "Have you sequenced other shifters, maybe those who aren't teetering on the brink of extinction?"

"Yeah." He waved a dismissive hand. "Mostly domesticated breeds, but I think that's barking up the wrong tree, if you'll pardon the expression. I know Amaricio married a dog shifter. A dog. *Pfft.*"

"He's really nice." Koren defended Edgar, and by extension, Chay. "They have offspring now, two sons and a daughter."

"A litter." Anshu's laugh was tinged with bitterness, and then it died away. When he spoke again, his voice was soft with yearning. "I bet they're happy."

"They are." Koren cleared his throat. "My omega is also a canine shifter. I think you're barking up the right tree. Dragons, pegasi, phoenixes—all the mythical shifters are dying out. We used to have booming populations, and now we've become fictional creatures in legends and fairy tales."

That gave Anshu pause. "These offspring—are they dogs or dragons?"

"I don't know," Koren admitted. "Dogs shift at six months, but dragons take substantially longer."

"You haven't tested their DNA?"

"Amar won't consent."

Anshu waved a hand. "What about your omega? Is he pregnant?"

"Not that I know of." They'd had sex a handful of times, not because Koren didn't want more, but because he'd been preoccupied with making sure he did his job so Tito stayed out of his personal life. Chay hadn't said anything, but then again, Koren hadn't spent enough time with him to give him a chance.

"You're going to need DNA samples from both parents and the offspring." Seemingly over the disappointment due to Koren's lack of romantic interest, Anshu's attention returned to science, which was where Koren felt the most comfortable. "I'd sneak them. You're friends. Offer to babysit. When they're gone, do a cheek swab. You don't have to tell Amaricio anything."

"That's unethical."

Anshu snorted. "Unethical. For fuck's sake, Koren, you've stolen research and tech from me for years. When did you suddenly get a sense of ethics?"

There was no point in denying it. "That's different. You're not one of my best friends."

"Only because you're narrow-minded." Anshu's mouth puckered in a sour pout. "Just like every other alpha out there."

Koren wasn't sure if he was supposed to defend all alphas or just the ones from his tribe. He glanced around. "I thought Lajos was going to be here?"

"I propositioned him, so he's avoiding me."

Six months ago, if Anshu had propositioned him, Koren wouldn't have turned him down. "That's unfortunate."

"Here's what I want," Anshu said. "I want an alpha. You find me a willing alpha, and I'll share my research."

This was outside Koren's realm of experience. He was not well-versed in romantic interactions. "Wouldn't you feel better if you found someone yourself?"

"I'm not talking about a mate. I'm talking about someone willing to show me a good time for a night or even a weekend." Anshu got to his feet and gestured to the door. "You have my number."

Though the plane ticket that would take him to a small airport in the Canadian Rockies was in his pocket, Koren returned home. He'd reschedule his meeting with the Rock-Shapers for another time. Amar had been right to point out Koren's now-or-never approach was a function of panic and obsession, and not a response to reality.

Tito might be pressuring him to solve a problem affecting the future of all dragonkind—and Koren felt the weight of that pressure—but the issue could keep for the time being.

If he hurried, he could still make the reservation Chay had scheduled.

Chapter 12—Chay

Chay smiled across the table at his sisters. Felicity and Bette were both pretty women, and anyone seeing them with Chay could easily discern they were siblings. They had a familial look about them, and when they were together, their genuine smiles spoke to the depth of their shared affection.

"I researched Verdance," Felicity said. "But I want to know from an insider's perspective—what's your favorite thing to do here?"

"I'm not much of an insider." Chay chuckled. "I've lived here a month. I've mostly been going through Uncle Chayton's stuff and working."

"Bartending?" Bette asked.

"Yes. I'll take you to Petrichor tomorrow. They have ladies' specials on Saturday nights." Chay thought about what he liked to do best, and it had nothing to do with the city. "My favorite thing to do is to go for runs after work. I usually work until about two-thirty or three, and then I take a detour on my way home to go for a run."

They knew, without him having to say, that he shifted for those runs.

Felicity leaned closer, a hint of worry etched on her forehead. "What about animal control? They have that here. It's not like at home, where you can gallivant all over the place and nobody cares."

They'd grown up in a dog-friendly town, but shifters lived all over the place. Though he hadn't been enthusiastic about coming to Verdance, he could admit that he was enjoying the experience.

Mostly.

Having an alpha who was constantly busy with other things sucked.

"Is this seat taken?"

His thought to explain about Verdance's history of being a home to shifters arrested, Chay followed the surprised gazes of his sisters to find Koren standing behind the empty chair next to him. Reflexively, he rose. "I thought you were out of town for a meeting."

"I came back." Koren smiled softly, his words heavy with meaning. It was an apology and an acknowledgment of sorts. He leaned down, smacking a kiss on Chay's lips before Chay could say anything more. "I missed you."

Tender feelings swelled in Chay's heart. He'd missed Koren as well, but not just tonight. That empty feeling had become part and parcel of being in a relationship with a workaholic.

Choked with emotion, Chay struggled to remember his manners. He opened his mouth, but he'd temporarily forgotten how to form words.

Koren came to the rescue. He reached across the table, offering his hand. "I'm Koren. You must be Felicity."

Felicity's brows rose. "Good guess. Hi, Koren. It's great to meet you."

"Not a guess," Koren returned. "Chay has pictures of you in his apartment." He reached out toward Bette. "Hi, Bette. It's a pleasure to meet you as well. Chay has told me so much about both of you."

Bette laughed. "You'd think he'd find more interesting things to talk about."

Koren seated Chay, and then he sat as well. He slung his arm around the back of Chay's chair. "Family is extremely important to Chay, and talking about you all helps him feel less homesick."

Though Chay had chattered on about his siblings and fathers at length, mostly while preparing a meal, he'd never been sure Koren was listening.

Chay knew Bette was in favor of his relationship with Koren and Felicity would be the harder sell, and Felicity didn't disappoint. She waited until the server brought a menu for Koren and took his drink order before pouncing. "Is family important to you?"

Koren's fingers played along the collar of Chay's shirt. "I'm an only child, and my parents still live in Turkey, so I don't see them often. My friends here have become my family, and they are all very important to me. When Chay and I get married, you'll be my family as well."

They hadn't discussed marriage. Chay stared at Koren. "You haven't asked me to marry you."

"I'm waiting until I'm certain you'll say yes." Koren thanked the server for bringing the beer he'd ordered. All the while, his fingers traced paths on Chay's shirt, slipping up every few seconds to caress his exposed skin.

Chay realized he would probably turn Koren down. Though they'd been together for a month, Koren had spent the majority of that time working. While Chay had powerful feelings for Koren, and he didn't doubt Koren felt the same way about him, he wasn't jazzed about the idea of being a forgotten spouse.

"Good call," he agreed.

Koren favored him with an apologetic smile. "What do you have planned for tonight?"

"After dinner, we were going to walk around, maybe go to a karaoke bar." He hadn't discussed the idea with Felicity or Bette, but he knew they both liked silly singing. Mostly he'd thrown it out there because he didn't think it was the kind of thing Koren would like to do. Except on their picnic date, he'd never seen his alpha cut loose and have fun.

He wasn't even sure Koren liked music. Every time he turned on the radio in Koren's kitchen, it was tuned to stations that featured talk shows.

To his surprise, Koren's grin turned playful. "I don't mind cheering for you."

Bette snorted, drawing them out of their flirty bubble. "You're required to get up there at least once."

"You might regret that," Koren warned. "I'm tone deaf."

Felicity laughed. "Then you're stuck with Bette. Chay and I will do a duet together because we don't suck."

The night flew past in a symphony of conversation and laughter. Except when he couldn't, Koren held Chay's hand or found ways to constantly touch him. At the karaoke bar, Bette and Koren slaughtered a Bee Gees song to the point where there was no discernible melody. Chay and Felicity did a passable version of *Islands in the Stream*, but that was kind of cheating because it was a song they'd performed together once at a talent show that raised money for an animal rehabilitation clinic.

In the hall in front of his apartment, Chay shooed his sisters inside and closed the door. Before he could say a word, Koren devoured his lips in a hungry kiss that finished atoning for their disagreement that morning.

When it ended, Koren held him close. "I want to ask you to come upstairs with me, but I know you probably want more time with your sisters."

Chay rested his cheek against Koren's shoulder. "You came all the way back here just to spend the evening with me."

"Yeah, well, I've been a neglectful boyfriend."

"And you listened to me. I never knew if you were paying attention. Sometimes I said stuff just to see if you'd respond, and you almost never did." Chay knew that Koren wasn't much of a talker, and he'd carried entire conversations on his own.

Koren brushed his fingers through Chay's hair. "I always listen when you talk, but sometimes it takes me a while to process, especially when I'm preoccupied. I'm a thinker. A lot of the time, I think of things to say, but by then you're long gone and I'm at work."

"You can call me," Chay offered. "I'd rather hear from you later than never."

A somberness settled over Koren that had a streak of fear hammering in Chay's chest, and that trepidation only increased when Koren eased back a step. "Chay, I need you to tell me when I'm doing things wrong. This is new to me—falling in love and having to worry about someone other than myself. I've come to realize I'm not a natural at being a good boyfriend."

Chay let the weight of the moment wash over him. Canine alphas tended to be reasonable most of the time. He hadn't known what to expect from a dragon, and it looked like Koren didn't have all the answers either. He was relieved to find out Koren was the kind of man who could admit his limitations.

Then Chay's playful side took over. He cupped the bulge between Koren's legs and rubbed lightly, urging the cock to grow. "A good boyfriend would kiss his omega goodnight and go home. A great boyfriend would take his omega home and show him how much he loves him. Are you aiming for good or great tonight?"

Koren's eyes lit, and the intense aura around him flared brightly. "Would a great boyfriend let you go inside and say goodnight to your sisters, or would he throw your ass over his shoulder and carry you up the stairs?"

Given the winks and elbow nudges Bette had been throwing his way all evening, he knew his sisters would figure out where he'd gone. Licking his lips, Chay's desire-roughened voice croaked, "Stairs."

In a blink, Koren's shoulder lined up with Chay's midsection, and then he found himself lifted. Koren's long legs ate the distance to the stairwell, and he took the stairs three at a time. It wasn't the most comfortable ride, but Chay didn't care. He'd slipped firmly into omega headspace, and his canine whined, begging to be taken by his alpha.

Koren didn't stop until they reached his bedroom, and Chay found himself bouncing on the pillowy mattress. Before he could think of something licentious to say, Koren's mouth captured his in a demanding kiss while his body pressed Chay's into the softness of the thick comforter.

He moaned and arched, wanting to be even closer to Koren. Clothing that had been soft and stylish an hour ago chaffed his skin. He tugged at Koren's shirt with one hand and unknit the zipper of Koren's jeans with the other.

With a husky chuckle, Koren broke the fathomless kiss. He trailed his hand between them, and Chay's shirt fell away. With a gasp, he looked down to see that Koren's hand had morphed into a talon, and he used his razor-sharp claw to slice through Chay's clothes. He traced a talon from Chay's neck to his belly before cutting down the arms of the garment. The pliant material gave way to gravity and fell to the bed.

Next, Koren attacked Chay's pants. He'd donned his best cargo pants, the ones that made his ass look exceptionally delicious, and now he watched as Koren shredded them. The talon's tip tickled against his skin, scraping an erotic path and leaving Chay trembling with need.

Koren's gaze followed where his talon went, flicking up occasionally to monitor Chay's reaction. His irises had transformed to the reptilian slits they became when he was aroused. "You like this," he noted.

"Yes," Chay said. He knew that one wrong move would leave him with cuts, and he found the imminent danger utterly thrilling. His cock throbbed, and he wondered if he could come just from being touched like this.

"Don't move," Koren cautioned. "There's nothing sharper than a dragon's claw."

"I figured that out when you sliced through my clothes like a hot knife through butter." Every inch Koren touched blazed with aching fire.

"Do you trust me?"

"Would I be letting you do this if I didn't?"

"You might just be terrified I'll kill you."

If anyone else had said that, Chay would have taken it as a threat. But he knew Koren didn't intend for him to be afraid, and he wasn't out to hurt him. "I'm not afraid of you. The trembling is because I'm so fucking turned on that I'm seconds from spilling my load."

A smile curved Koren's lips. "You like risk."

"Seems like." Chay would agree with anything Koren said as long as he didn't stop the unexpectedly erotic edge play.

"You shift at night and go running without anyone to keep watch. A million things could happen to you, and yet when you return, you're refreshed and calm."

Except that first day, Chay had kept his three-in-the-morning runs to himself. After tending bar, he carefully hid his clothes in a backpack in an alley, explored until he was tired, and then he returned to his clothes. He dressed hurriedly and went home. The entire exercise took an hour or two.

Shock doused some of the pleasure taking over Chay's mind. He stared at Koren. "How do you know that?"

"By accident. A couple weeks ago, I was coming home from work late. It was a little after closing time, and so I flew over Petrichor, hoping to catch you." He drew the flat of his claw along Chay's collarbone and across his neck. At the notch under his Adam's apple, Koren pressed the sharp tip of his claw into Chay's skin. "And I did. I caught you, naughty puppy. Most nights you work, I'm in the sky, flying above you and keeping watch. A few times when I couldn't, I had Zeke or Eli do it."

Chay struggled not to swallow. The smallest movement could result in a deep cut. A million questions ran through his head, but they disappeared when Koren's mouth closed over his cock. He sucked hard, pumping his head up and down, and then he released it with a loud, smacking sound.

The talon moved down.

"You never said if you trusted me." Koren knelt on either side of Chay's hips, his weight causing Chay's ass to dip down into the crease.

Koren dragged his talon through the sparse hairs on Chay's chest, and he circled a nipple.

"I trust you," Chay promised. "With everything I have."

Koren played with Chay's nipples, circling until they were hard nubs, and then he flicked the tips, scratching them with the rough and sharp edge of his talons. Chay realized different parts of Koren's talon had different textures, though they were sharp all over.

The pinprick sensations on his nipples ripped a moan from his depths, and he struggled not to arch into it. He gripped Koren's thighs, digging his fingers into the iron flesh to keep from writhing.

Koren's caress moved lower, and he scooted so that he pinned Chay's thighs in place. "I'm going to touch your cock with my talon. It's your job not to move, and the only way you're going to be successful is if you trust me."

"I trust you." This time, it came out a little louder and more resolute. "And I'm pretty sure I'm going to orgasm if you do that."

"As long as you don't move." Koren chuckled, a hint of devilry in his tone.

Chay reached up and held onto the spindles in Koren's headboard. Koren gripped Chay's cock in his human hand, and he drew the tip of his talon across Chay's sac.

A moan issued from Chay. What Koren was doing was hot, and being forced to keep still only ramped up the heat of passion.

Koren played with his balls for a bit, alternating using his hand and his talon. Then he ran the sharp tip of his talon up the underside of Chay's cock. Molten heat curled Chay's toes and traveled up his body. Before he made it to the crown, an orgasm detonated. His entire body stiffened as his eyes rolled back in his head. He didn't mean to move, but he knew he had.

From the lack of pain, he deduced that his trust in Koren had not been misplaced. The world was black because his vision had not returned, and he felt little flutters on his belly. When everything came into focus, he saw Koren leaning over his midsection, lapping up every drop of ejaculate.

When he finished, he glanced up at Chay. A cocky smile stole over his features. "Welcome back, my naughty risk-taker."

"That was amazing. I've never experienced anything like it."

Koren's lips plundered his, and Chay tasted his semen on his alpha's tongue. The curiously erotic mix made him feel even more subservient to his alpha. He wanted—needed—to feel Koren inside him. Wordlessly his canine whined, begging to be taken.

Breaking the kiss, Koren sat back on his heels. "Hands and knees, Chay. I'm not going to be gentle."

He didn't want gentle. He wanted to be claimed and owned. Scrambling to obey, Chay offered himself to his alpha.

Koren pushed his head down, smashing his cheek to the comforter, and he nudged Chay's knees wider. This position left him completely at Koren's mercy, and Chay loved every second of it. He felt wetness coat his anus, and then the thick head of Koren's cock prodded his opening.

"Exhale."

With that single-word order, Koren reamed him. Though he'd obeyed, he still cried out from the sheer force of the act. Without waiting for him to acclimate, Koren set a furious pace. His fingers dug into Chay's hips as he held him still.

White-hot pleasure burned from Chay's spine. With every deep thrust and the slap of Koren's balls against his, Chay's cock hardened. Nothing compared to the feeling of being filled by his alpha, and Koren's passionate cries multiplied every sensation.

With a mighty roar and the throwing of flames, Koren's hot seed spilled into Chay. He collapsed on top of his omega, and Chay lay there, cocooned in the warm embrace of the man he loved.

Minutes passed, and their bodies cooled. Chay looked up to see burn marks singeing the wall. He giggled.

"What's funny?" Koren didn't move or open his eyes, but he did roll to the side so Chay could breathe.

"You scorched the wall."

Koren cracked an eye, taking in the damage. "Your job to redecorate."

"Because I'm an omega, you assume I'm going to take over household responsibilities?"

"Pretty much."

He smacked Koren's chest. "This is your house, not mine."

Koren caught his hand and brushed a kiss on his knuckles. "For now. It'll keep."

It would keep.

Chay rolled over and adjusted the pillows behind him. Then he palmed his cock, which responded by lengthening.

Koren glanced over. "For real? You just came."

"I'm twenty-four, and I'm a dog shifter. We're randy fuckers."

"Masturbate," Koren ordered. "I want to watch."

Under the totally hot and observant gaze of his alpha, Chay pumped his hand up and down his shaft. He'd done this a million times, but there was something about having Koren watch that made it that much hotter.

"Don't come."

Chay's hand stuttered. "What?"

"I didn't say to stop." Koren grinned. "Just don't come."

"That's not fair."

"Life's not fair." Koren went to his dresser and opened a drawer. He returned with a small leather strap, which he tied around Chay's cock and balls. "Keep masturbating."

Chay stroked his cock much less vigorously.

Koren watched for a while, and then he pushed Chay's hands out of the way. He closed his mouth over Chay's erection. That familiar heat, which had become a hollow act lately, took on a new urgency. Koren worked his jaw rhythmically, and the heat inside grew. It was enough to drive him up the cliff, but not enough to cause harm.

Before long, a pins-and-needles feeling suffused his limbs. He writhed and cried out. With his mighty, preternatural strength, Koren held down Chay's pelvis and legs.

Chay wanted very badly to come. He willed his climax to happen, but it didn't. Held off by that dastardly strap, the earthquake gathered force. When it broke, when it finally broke, white-hot flames shot through his body, and the climax rocked him to the core. He didn't remember anything after that.

In the morning, he woke in Koren's arms. The alpha's legs were twined with his, and he held Chay tightly against his chest.

Tilting his head, Chay studied his lover's handsome face. Asleep, the intense air of energy Koren always carried was gone. In its place was a calm, peaceful man whose wild hair framed his face like a sinful halo. His wide shoulders peeked out above the comforter. Covered in long ropes of sinewy muscle, he didn't seem like an egghead. Geek. Nerd.

His alpha was a bona-fide nerd, and Chay found that fact as arousing as everything else about Koren.

Giving in to instinct, he licked a path up Koren's chest and neck, and he nipped at his alpha's ear.

Koren's eyes opened the slightest bit. "What are you doing?"

"I'm a biter," Chay admitted as he pinched small bites down Koren's neck. "Surprise."

"Feels good." Koren managed a growly, sleepy chuckle. "Just don't bite my cock."

"Can I suck it?"

"You can try."

Chay recalled the impossible thickness and how he'd only been able to get a few inches into his mouth. Reasoning the crown was the most sensitive point, he figured a few inches was enough.

Biting and licking his way down Koren's body, he took his lover's cock in his mouth. Soon small purrs of pleasure sounded in Koren's chest and vibrated his body. Encouraged by that reaction, Chay got serious.

Koren let him play for a while, and then he pulled Chay's head away from his cock.

Looking up with question in his eyes, Chay noted the telltale slits in Koren's eyes.

"It's slick enough. Ride me."

Obeying his alpha, Chay straddled Koren's cock, lining it up with his opening. He sank down slowly, controlling the depth and pace. He rode Koren's cock, and the alpha's large paw closed over Chay's cock, masturbating him as he fucked himself on that wide cock.

It didn't take long for orgasm to claim them both. They came together, Koren's semen emptying into Chay's body while Chay's spilled onto Koren's stomach.

"I like waking up this way," Koren said as he lifted Chay and carried him into the bathroom. "Let's shower, and then we can take your sisters to breakfast. I heard there was a street fair or something downtown today."

Chay started. Given the schedule Koren usually followed, he hadn't expected that his lover would join him for more than a meal or two. "You're sure you want to come along?"

Koren had been adjusting the water temperature. He backed out of the shower and leveled an knowing look at Chay. "Unless you don't want me to? I understand if you want some alone time with your sisters."

"No, it's just I thought you had to work."

Koren shrugged. "Work can wait. It's the weekend, and I've turned over a new leaf, one where I'm not a jerk to my omega."

Floored, Chay realized Koren meant what he said. A tear leaked from his eye.

Catching it, Koren took Chay in his arms. "Did I say the wrong thing?"

"No," Chay said. "You're perfect. I love you."

Tenderness softened Koren's hard features. "I love you too."

Chapter 13

Koren

Riding waves of euphoria brought on by the best weekend he'd ever experienced, Koren strode into his sixth floor lab at Draco International ready to work.

His rainbow attitude crashed when it noticed Tito Kaysar sitting behind his desk.

With his smile gone, Koren lifted his chin in a reluctant greeting. "Tito, did we have an appointment?"

"Yes." The large shifter leaned forward and folded his hands on the scraps of notes Koren had left on his desk. His actual notes were kept under lock and key.

For the first time since Friday, Koren remembered he had set up a meeting with representatives from the Rock-Shaper Tribe on Saturday. He'd completely forgotten about it. "Whoops."

Tito's brows lifted in mild irritation. "Whoops? That's all you have to say? You stood up a potential ally to spend your time with a man and two women. Who are they?"

Working until exhaustion had the built-in benefit of throwing Tito off the scent of Koren's omega—though, due to Koren's testimony, Tito had to know he had one. Koren set his briefcase on the desk and pulled out his notebooks. "None of your business."

"You kissed the man," Tito said. "Please tell me he's not a canine shifter."

"He's not a canine shifter," Koren repeated.

"Fuck." Kaysar let his head drop back in a dramatic display of exasperation. "I guess this underscores the urgency of you looking into canine shifters. Did you get anything from Anshu Bray?"

"He's a virgin." Koren hadn't meant to share that caveat with anyone, but it popped out unbidden. His subconscious apparently wanted to throw his boss off Chay's tail by giving him something equally juicy and yet unrelated.

Tito's mouth opened and closed. "Yes, well, that's neither here nor there." Then he frowned. "A virgin? Really?"

"I know. You'd think having the lone omega under fifty years old, the Ice-Breathers would be all over him, but they're not. They won't even fool around with him." Taking a chance, he motioned for Tito to vacate his chair.

Distracted by the new intel, Tito got up and moved out of the way. "I don't understand. He should be revered. He should have his choice of anyone he wants. This explains why he was so easy to persuade to give Amaricio a chance."

"Why not you?" Koren threw out that question because he was honestly interested in the answer. Of them all, Tito would be the one who was selfish enough to insist on continuing his bloodline.

Tito shook his head. "I didn't find him attractive in the least."

"He's handsome." Koren encouraged Tito to follow this data path.

"Without question." Plopping onto a less comfortable chair, Tito stroked his chin while he thought. "This is huge, Tafari. I wonder what else we'd know if you kept your appointment with the Rock-Shapers?"

"I'll reschedule that meeting," Koren said. "There is no hurry. Just as we do, they lack omegas. However, they also eschew modern research techniques."

"I know, but there is truth in the old ways. If anyone can glean something from nothing, it's you." As he had a thousand times before, he gazed at Koren as a proud patriarch. "You have a gift for separating science from sentiment. I hope this newfound association you've made doesn't change what I consider to be your best quality."

Long after Tito had left, Koren stared at his notes. He did have a habit of separating science from sentiment because objective facts and solid science were the keys to discovering new facets to the physical universe. He'd invented polymers and binding agents that led to revolutions in science and industry. Because he was a dragon shifter whose lifespan lasted hundreds of years, his role had been anonymous, and Draco International owned most of his work.

Even now, his brain was separating his feelings for Chay from the task of figuring out what the fuck was happening to his species. As the gears in his mind labored, Koren wondered whether this objectivity made him a good person or a bad one.

Chay was a good person. He was the kind of man who never waffled when it came to choosing to do the right thing. Friendly, generous, and loyal, he represented everything good in this world.

So why was part of Koren still considering sequencing his DNA for study, and later doing the same thing to any children they might have together?

What did that say about him? And—should he tell Chay about this shady side of his personality?

He honestly didn't know.

Chay

Monday, Koren came home from work distracted. The attentive boyfriend had lasted for a weekend, and Chay wondered if Koren had been putting on a show for his sisters.

It had worked. Before they'd left, each of his sisters had sought him out to give Koren their stamp of approval. Felicity promised to explain everything to Basil because Chay still couldn't bring himself to tell his brother he'd broken his promise to go slow and not fall in love with the first guy who kissed him in Verdance.

Chay had done exactly that.

Now, as he bopped around Koren's kitchen singing along with a 90's music station, he paused in considering what to make for dinner in order to study Koren.

His alpha sat on a high stool at the counter, staring at the middle distance while his mind seemed a million miles away.

Chay whirled to a stop opposite him and rested his elbows on the counter. "Want to talk about it?"

It took a few seconds, but Koren's gaze focused. It roamed Chay's features. "Do you think I'm a good person?"

Caught by surprise, Chay felt his brows lift and his mouth open. "Of course."

"But you have no way of knowing that," he pressed. "You haven't known me all that long."

"No, but I have a great sixth sense when it comes to picking out who is good and who isn't." Chay leaned closer and whispered conspiratorially. "It's a dog thing."

The flirtatious tone didn't seem to register with Koren. The corners of his mouth turned down. "I'm about to do something that a close friend has forbidden me from doing."

"Ah, a crisis of conscience." Chay slid onto the stool next to Koren and held his hands. "I'm listening."

Koren took forever to respond. Chay was glad that his alpha had shared the insight about how he tended to think through everything.

To Chay's way of seeing it, he was there to prevent Koren from overthinking.

At last, Koren sighed. "I need DNA samples from Amar, Edgar, and the babies. They invited us over for dinner tonight, and I was going to sneak it because Amar told me under no circumstances were his children being part of this study Kaysar has me doing."

Knowing the history behind Amar's reticence, Chay nodded. "Have you thought of asking again? Sometimes people change their minds."

Heaving a sigh, Koren ruffled his hair. "If I ask him and he refuses, he'll watch me the rest of the night, and I won't get a sample. I'd say there's an almost certain chance he'll refuse."

Chay chewed the inside of his lip as he thought. "You know, there's always plan B."

"Stealing the DNA is my plan B."

"No, silly." Chay released his hold on Koren's hand and spread his arms wide. "Me."

Koren blinked. "Have kids with you and use their DNA?"

The idea gave Chay tingles up and down his spine. He wanted to shout a resounding YES. "If you want, but that's down the road a few months. If you need it now, I can get the samples. They'd never suspect me."

"Why would you—Wait. A few months? Are you pregnant now?" Koren seemed both excited and perplexed. "I don't know how these things work."

Laughing, Chay said, "When two men love each other, that love opens up a mystical portal. Then the alpha's sperm travels through it to where the omega's eggs are stored. The sperm fertilizes the egg, and then babies form. After sixty-three days of growing inside a special pouch, they are ready to be born. Or whelped, as my fathers like to say."

A myriad thoughts seemed to go through Koren's mind, and Chay watched them churn. He found the transparency of the whole thing rather fascinating. Finally, Koren settled on an observation. "You didn't say whether you were pregnant or not."

Chay shrugged. "I don't think so. I mean, we aren't in the habit of using protection, but I'm fairly certain you meant it when you said you loved me."

"I did, but that—that's what makes conception possible?" He sprang from the stool and paced to the slider and back. "Could it be so simple? No. There are too many species that procreate without emotional involvement. That can't be the key. But then why—I don't know why it would matter." He said other things. Chay listened without interrupting. He meant to mention that he hadn't gone into heat, so pregnancy was highly unlikely, but Koren definitely wasn't listening right then.

When Koren settled down, Chay set his hands on his alpha's chest. "Explain how dragons have babies."

"Same story, except with laying eggs instead of live birth. Edgar had live births."

"Dogs do." Chay rubbed soothing circles on Koren's chest. "And shifters have never shared physiology with beings who don't shift. We're part magic. We're the supernatural. Different rules. Love matters among our kinds."

"My parents love each other very much," Koren said. "It doesn't explain the lack of births."

"But it's part of the equation." Chay widened his forays. "Koren, it doesn't make you a bad person for needing a scientific explanation for what's happening to dragonkind. It makes you *you*."

Gears turned, and it was sexy. Watching Koren puzzle through an issue made Chay's dick jerk.

"Okay," Koren said. "Now tell me why you'd be willing to let me lead you down a dishonest path."

Chay and Bas both had a playful nature—all Labs did—that had landed them in hot water many times. They'd never done anything reckless, but neither of them had an issue with walking the line or playing practical jokes. This kind of slight-of-hand was right up his alley.

Snorting, Chay laughed. "Koren, you seem to be laboring under the impression I'm innocent or angelic or something. Pretty much every night, I strip naked and run through the city. I knock over trash cans and mark my territory when people have annoyed me. A few nights ago, I orgasmed from edge play. Maybe take a moment and let that sink in. I don't mind being naughty with you. Also, I'm going to need a new pair of cargo pants before we go."

An hour later, Chay exclaimed over babies. Edgar's trio were freaking adorable. They were only a couple months old, and they were still tiny.

"Chay, meet Seth, Brendan, and Sarah Michelle." Edgar hovered over his children, a proud father beaming as someone else fawned over his accomplishments.

"Hi, babies. You are all so darn cute. Look at those tiny faces. And their hands—oh, I just love when babies grasp onto my fingers. It makes my heart sing." Most of Chay's gushing was real.

Behind them, Koren stood with Amar, both of them watching their omegas more than the babies.

Chay glanced back. He knew he sported a goofy grin because he was thinking about how great it would be to have children of his own. "Aren't you going to come see your niece and nephews?"

Koren gestured with uncharacteristic nervousness. "I don't really know anything about babies. I'm fine over here."

"You're not seriously going to avoid them?" Chay parked his hands on his hips. When Koren didn't move, Chay huffed his disapproval. "Koren Tafari, if you plan on having kids, then you're going to need to get over your fear of small creatures. Come over here and hold one of these precious babies."

Edgar giggled, and he picked up Seth. "Amar didn't know anything about babies either, but he wasn't squeamish." He handed Seth to his alpha.

Next, he handed Brendan to Chay, and he took Sarah Michelle. "Let's go into the living room. Koren can get the drinks, and I have appetizers on the counter."

In the living room, Chay selected a loveseat, and patted the place next to him. Having a baby so close in proximity would help Koren acclimate. Chay listened as Edgar chattered about fatherhood and how wonderful Amar was. Interspersed with those were mentions of Koren that kept Chay's attention.

During dinner, things got hectic. As soon as they all sat down to eat the scrumptious meal Edgar had prepared, Sarah Michelle let loose with an angry wail.

To Chay's surprise, Amar rushed to her side. They'd set the babies in swings where they could see their fathers and each other. He scooped up his daughter. "What's wrong, sweetheart? Let Daddy fix it."

She paused, huge tears shimmering in her eyes, and peered at Amar. Then she leaned forward and snuggled into his shoulder.

Edgar chuckled. "She has him firmly wrapped around her finger. That girl is a diva in training, and by that, I mean she's the diva, and Amar is the one being trained."

"She just likes to be held," Amar protested.

Through it all, Koren remained slightly dazed. Chay let him stay that way until Seth and Brendan demanded the same treatment as Sarah Michelle. Both boys registered protest cries at the same time.

Chay rose, and put a hand on Edgar's shoulder. "You spent all this time slaving away over a hot stove. How about you enjoy the meal? Koren and I will tend to the boys."

Quashing Koren's protest, Chay plopped Brendan in his lap, and he took Seth.

A huge smile split Seth's face, and he flapped his arms while squealing with glee. Over on Koren's lap, Brendan stared up at his uncle with wide eyes. The pair studied one another, neither saying a word. After a few quiet moments, a huge smile broke out on Brendan's face, and it was echoed on Koren's.

"Chay, you seem like you've been around lots of babies. I thought Koren said you were a youngest child?" Edgar ended by shoveling a huge spoonful of mashed potatoes into his mouth.

"I am," Chay shared. "My brother, Basil, and I were the second litter. But I have tons of cousins, and there were always babies around in our neighborhood growing up. Kids like me, babies especially, and I've done a ton of babysitting. I thought about becoming a nanny, but people are weird about a guy who likes children, as if there's something wrong with men who enjoy nurturing the next generation."

Next to him, Koren's brows lifted. "You wanted to be a nanny, but you became a bartender instead? Why not a teacher?"

The idea of attending school ever again didn't sit well with Chay. "I wasn't a great student. I like people, but not studying."

"You read all the time," Koren said. "I've seen books in your apartment from the library, and you borrow mine."

Chay loved to read. He just hated tests, papers, and worksheets.

"And you're really smart," Koren continued. "When I talk about work, you keep up with what I'm saying just fine."

Fluttering his lashes, he said, "If any of my teachers were as sexy and interesting as you, I might have been a better student. But it's not my thing. I've always wanted to be a stay-at-home dad like mine was. Bartending is fun because I get to meet people and talk to them—and the more they drink, the more they talk. It's fun."

"I loved my job as a personal assistant," Edgar said. "But I think my boss may have fired me."

"I didn't fire you." Annoyance crept into Amar's tone, but he tempered it when Sarah Michelle hiccupped. "You're on paternity leave."

"Unpaid," Edgar snorted.

"Good thing you're married to an alpha who sees to your every need." From the way Edgar's eyes widened, Amar must have done something fun and risqué under the table.

While they were engaged in that activity, Chay took the opportunity to swab Seth's cheek. He had the evidence safely tucked into the deep pocket of his cargo pants before anyone noticed. He didn't even know if Koren had caught his action.

Within the next hour, he managed to get swabs from Brendan and Sarah Michelle.

Conversation flowed, and after dinner was cleaned up, Edgar and Amar disappeared to put the babies to bed.

Chay snuggled into Koren's side and kissed his alpha. "I thought you did very well with Seth. He liked you."

"He's cute," Koren said. "And so small. I was afraid I'd break him."

"The more you handle babies, the more confident you'll get." Chay nipped at Koren's bottom lip.

Koren captured his mouth in a gentle kiss. "Chay, did you mean it when you said you wanted to be a househusband?"

The whole evening, Chay had been brash and friendly. Now shyness crept over him. "Yeah. It's stupid, I know. But my dad was always there for us, available for anything, and it was really nice knowing he was there. It's not like my father wasn't, but he worked, and having my dad at home made everything—I don't know—better. I grew up in a happy home, and I want my kids to have the same thing."

"So do I." Koren's steady gaze grew sober, and the intensity of his blue eyes bound Chay better than a rope. "Marry me. I love you, Chay. I want to give you everything your heart desires. You can quit your job and devote your life to taking care of me and the ten kids we're going to have."

"Ten?" Chay laughed nervously. "That's a lot. Let's start with a litter and see what happens."

Koren's expression turned pensive. "Is that a yes?"

"Yes." Throwing his arms around Koren, Chay climbed onto his lap. "That's definitely a yes."

The ensuing kiss was not at all gentle. It was hard and possessive, an alpha claiming his omega.

"Oh, did I overhear what I think I heard?" From the opening that led to the hallway, Edgar clapped his hands. "Can I say congratulations?"

"Edgar, let them have a moment." Amar's growl carried back to them as he whisked his omega away.

Chay dimly heard all that as the explosive kiss stole his breath and rendered him boneless.

A few minutes later, armed with fluted glasses and champagne, Edgar crept back into the room. Amar trailed in his wake.

"Can we do a toast before you rush back home to have celebratory sex?" Edgar set the glasses down. "Please? I'm so happy for you guys."

"Absolutely." Koren set Chay back on the sofa, but Chay didn't go far. He kept his thigh pressed to Koren's. "But we're not taking off so soon. I wanted to talk to you both about something first."

"Okay." Bubbling over with enthusiasm, Edgar poured the drinks.

Chay noticed that, while Amar seemed genuinely happy for them, his expression was guarded. He was gearing up for a confrontation. A glance at Edgar showed he was also aware of the change in Amar's mood. Dogs always knew when danger was brewing.

Edgar distributed the drinks and raised his glass. "Congratulations to Koren and Chay. We wish you love and happiness, and we're hoping for a few cousins and lots of playdates."

"Thank you, Edgar and Amar." Koren slung his arm around Chay's shoulders. "I'm not sure we'd be here today without you. Amar, you inspired and encouraged me to go for it with Chay, and Edgar, you provided lots of support and a new wardrobe that made me look good enough to keep Chay's attention."

Chay drank to the toast, and then he peered at Koren, taking in the stylish shirt that emphasized the powerful blue of his eyes and the rather plain jeans that cupped his ass perfectly. "A new wardrobe? How do you normally dress?"

"Now I dress like this." Koren's mouth set in a mulish slant.

"Messy," Amar said. "He was the epitome of a mad scientist who didn't care what he looked like under his lab coat. Go through his closet. I bet he hasn't cleared out the old stuff."

"Now would be a great time for you to stop talking, Amar." Koren glared.

Edgar giggled. "What was he wearing when you met?"

Thinking back, Chay recalled the worn, stained shirt and the small holes in the ill-fitting jeans. He'd been more concerned with the way his canine reacted than in those unimportant details. Later that day, he'd shown up with a new haircut and fresh clothes, and Chay had chalked up the earlier outfit to a messy project at work.

Chay played with a lock of Koren's shoulder-length hair. "I was too busy getting lost in his eyes to notice."

"You're welcome." Edgar sat down with a smug expression on his face.

"Now that we've resolved that mystery, what was this important thing you wanted to discuss?" Amar downed the contents of his glass, and then he set it on the table next to his chair. "And it better not be a request for DNA from Edgar or my children."

Koren leaned forward. "Hear me out, Grange. I have good reasons."

Amar's face darkened, and as he was rather swarthy already, his skin took on a ruddy undertone. "I don't give a fuck what your reasons are. Tito Kaysar will not get his hands on anything related to me or mine."

"I wish you two wouldn't fight." Edgar perched on the arm of Amar's chair and set his hand on his alpha's shoulder. "You're on the same side."

"I'm not sure that's true," Amar said. "Koren has thrown himself into this research project. In one short month, he's managed to become one of the most knowledgeable people in the world on the subject."

"I wouldn't say that," Koren hedged.

"Tito spent a lot of money on equipment for your new lab." Dead calm and danger emanated from Amar. "All the invoices go through me, Koren. I know you're preparing to sequence DNA so you can study and isolate genetic differences."

This was news to Chay. He peered at Koren, who owed the next answer.

"Look, I didn't ask for this assignment. At first, I was pissed to have it thrust upon me, but the more I learned, the better I understood why we need these answers."

Amar shook his head. "I don't care, Koren. None of that matters to me. Tito kidnapped my omega and subjected him to medical testing. He planned to keep my children from me. That is unforgivable, and of all people, you should understand why I won't participate." He nodded to Chay. "Maybe you'll understand when you have kids of your own."

Next to him, anger and hurt vibrated from Koren. Though he didn't appear to have a reaction, Chay was in tune with is alpha. He knew the depth of the upset with which Koren was grappling.

Chay appealed to Edgar. "I know what happened to you, and I think it's horrible. I can't imagine the nightmares you must still have."

"No, you can't," Edgar said. "But they're easing. Having so much good in my life helps keep the worst of it at bay."

"I've given my DNA to Koren," Chay confided. "And when we have kids, he'll test theirs. I want to know as much as I can about them. I mean, how many dragon-dog hybrids are out there? I want to know if they're more dragon or dog. Dragon shifters live four times as long as dog shifters do. I want to know if that gets passed to my kids, or maybe it's some kind of genetic compromise? What are the dominant traits, and what kinds of problems might be down the road? I want to be prepared so I can be the best parent to my kids."

Amar's penetrating gaze burned figurative holes into Chay's head. He'd directed his speech to Edgar, hoping to sway the omega because he knew the omega held most of the real power in a relationship.

But on this issue, Edgar deferred to his alpha.

Amar's expression softened, but it remained resolute. "Look, I can understand your concerns and fears, but I cannot consent to this while Tito controls Draco International. I'm sorry, Koren, but the answer is still no."

Koren nodded. "I understand. Thank you for hearing us out."

Chay wasn't under the impression Koren had made half of his arguments, but he knew Amar's mind was made up. In true canine fashion, Chay beamed. "Okay, now that's out of the way. Edgar, you're going to have to show me where you bought Koren's clothes because what you said explains why he only has four shirts he wears."

Even Amar cracked a smile. "Make him marry you first."

"Well, that's going to take a while. I have to live in my apartment for another five months before I officially inherit it, and Koren won't move in with me. He likes his place better. It is better, but that doesn't change the terms of my uncle's will." He squeezed Koren's thigh to show that he wasn't upset.

The arm Koren had slung behind him bent, and a sharp point teased along the back of his neck. "We can combine them into one unit. We'll need the extra space if we're going to have a dozen kids."

Knowing better than to move, Chay remained frozen. "A dozen? At last count, we'd negotiated one litter with a contingency for a later conversation."

"Did we?" Koren flashed a wicked smile that promised a lopsided negotiation. The talon morphed back into a hand, but the element of sensual danger remained.

"We did." A shiver of anticipation traveled up Chay's spine.

"Okay," Edgar clapped his hands together and got to his feet. "You two probably want to get home to celebrate. Chay, I'll call you tomorrow and schedule a time to go shopping. I have to see when my sister can come over and babysit."

"Oh, you're welcome to bring the babies," Chay said, clasping his hands over his heart. "I don't mind at all."

Edgar's gaze flitted to Amar. "Maybe. Sometimes it's nice to get out without the kids, get a break. You know."

Chay remembered how his dad sometimes went fishing alone. He always came back rejuvenated. Of course, this might be a case of Edgar being leery of Chay because of Koren's request.

In the end, Chay and Edgar hugged goodbye, and Amar shook his hand.

Chay held Koren's hand as they walked back to their building.

"Want to go for a run?" Koren asked.

While that sounded like fun, especially if Koren wanted to come along, Chay wanted to expend his energies in other ways. "Maybe later."

"Thought I'd ask."

"Thanks."

They walked along in silence, their fingers intertwined. When they passed people on the sidewalk, Koren drew Chay closer to make room, pressing their bodies together.

In the elevator, Koren cleared his throat. "Chay, don't take this the wrong way, but you smell really, really good."

Laughter startled from Chay. "Is there a wrong way to take that?"

"I mean, like irresistibly good. Like 'my dragon wants to rip off your clothes and take you right now' good."

Chay exhaled hard. "Yeah. My heat is starting."

"Your heat?"

"A period of fertility where I emit pheromones designed to make my alpha sex-crazed so he'll impregnate me. Heat. All dogs have it, shifter or not." Chay rubbed his pelvis against Koren's thigh. "Maybe you want to wear a condom for the next week?"

Koren stared at the ceiling and his Adam's apple bobbed as he swallowed. "We'll visit the courthouse tomorrow and get a marriage license."

"You don't have to—"

"I want to." Koren squeezed a handful of Chay's ass. "But I can wait if you don't."

"Yeah, no. I'm fine." To help Koren stave off his baser urges, Chay withdrew three long vials from his largest pocket. "I got you something."

Koren's gaze dropped until it rested on the vials. "You swabbed their cheeks? When? I was with you the whole time, and I didn't see a thing."

"I'm fucking amazing," Chay explained. "You can spend the night rewarding me. I won't mind."

The elevator chimed, and Koren scooped Chay into his arms. "All night? I can do that."

Epilogue

Koren

Chay waddled into the nearly empty living room. He'd spent the last two months dispersing furniture to family and friends of his uncle, and now it held only the essentials. Koren's heart melted a little, the way it did every time he saw his pregnant husband.

"We should keep the kitchen," Koren said. "That way, we won't have to run up and down the stairs to heat bottles or get snacks."

Both of the apartments were large for a single person, but they were still two-bedroom domiciles. They planned to use the upstairs apartment as their living space, and the downstairs one would be dedicated to sleeping.

"Master suite, three additional bedrooms, and a small living room."

"Four additional bedrooms," Koren corrected. "And if we need to use all six for kids, then we can convert a room upstairs to a bedroom for us."

Chay rolled his eyes and stuck a carrot stick into his mouth. "Even though making them is so much fun, I'm not sold on raising a dozen kids."

"Work in progress." Koren wasn't deterred. He didn't know if he truly wanted that many kids, but he liked teasing Chay.

Another work in progress was the DNA samples Chay had taken from Amar's triplets as well as swabs from Chay and himself. Sequencing took a lot longer than any of them expected, and Koren anxiously awaited the results.

He also anxiously awaited the birth of his own children. Ultrasound scans showed twins.

"Wanna have sex?" Chay munched another carrot stick. "I'm horny."

The need Koren had to suck Chay's cock had not abated. It was rare that he skipped a day, but he'd woken up early that morning to get some work done. Chay was due tomorrow, and Koren had arranged to take time off as they acclimated to their new family.

On that front, they expected Chay's family to arrive at any moment.

"C'mon," Chay cajoled. "A quickie. You know you want me."

He very much did, but he stayed put.

Chay came closer. His leg brushed against Koren's, and he cupped the alpha's cock through his pants. "Mmm. That's quite a large problem you have, Mr. Tafari. I can help you with it."

Finished with the waiting game, Koren cupped the back of Chay's head and held him still for a kiss that sizzled to his toes. Though he held his omega near, Chay's hands were in motion, teasing, caressing, and unzipping.

By the time Koren ripped his mouth away, Chay's hot hands were around his cock.

"Drop your pants," Koren ordered. "Bend over the back of the sofa. Brace yourself."

Chay scrambled to get into position, and Koren met him there. As he sank into his omega, he reached around to stroke his lover's cock.

"We're going to come together, Chay."

"I'll give it my best shot."

Before Koren could counter, Chay cried out. Hot semen spilled over Koren's hand.

"Sorry, not sorry," Chay said. "I told you I was horny."

Koren licked the delicious and addictive fluid from his hand as he thrust into his lover. It didn't take him long to follow Chay into bliss. As his orgasm throbbed through him, he held Chay in his arms.

"I love you, my darling omega."

"I love you too, my sexy, alpha stud."

With a grin, Koren smacked Chay's ass. "Get dressed. I heard the elevator."

Chay

Labor was painful. He hadn't realized how much it would hurt before the harder contractions hit. He gripped Koren's hand as he screamed through the agony.

"You're doing great." Nilo, his dad, coached him through the contraction. "Push with the next one."

The whole family had come for this. Upstairs, his father, brothers, and sisters waited with Koren's fathers. Lizz was there as well. Their friendship had grown even moreso over the past couple of months. Amar and Edgar had come. Eli and Zeke had been called, but Chay had stopped keeping track by then.

Koren's lips pressed to his temple. "Almost there. You're being very brave."

"Fuck off," Chay said. "There's no way in hell I'm doing this a dozen times."

"I know." Koren's authoritative voice soothed the worst of Chay's nerves. "I was kidding."

"You weren't."

"I'm open to negotiation."

Before he could reply, another contraction hit, and he cried out.

"Push," Nilo said. "There's a head. Oh, and there's the rest." He set the baby on Chay's chest.

Chay counted fingers and toes, noting that he had a son. "Chayton Sadler the Sixth." He glared at Koren, daring him to object.

"Sure," Koren said. "Anything you want."

"Seventh," Nilo corrected. "Chayton Four beat you to the Sixth a few days ago."

"Fine. Chayton Sadler the Seventh."

"You know his last name is Tafari, right?" Koren wiped the baby down as they talked. "As is yours."

Chay glared. He was not in the mood for logic games. However, Koren didn't seem to be paying attention to anything but little Seven. And then iron bands squeezed out his insides.

"There's his brother," Nilo said as the infant slid into his hands. "Maybe Koren the Second?"

That sounded great to Chay. He grinned, and he threw that decision to Koren. "What do you think? We could start a new tradition."

"I think it's confusing to have so many people with the same name." Koren spoke bluntly. "Plus, Koren is a stupid name. I've always liked the idea of Leo."

"Then he's Leo." Chay lay back and closed his eyes as a wave of exhaustion swept over him. "But, for the record, I like your name a whole heck of a lot."

Koren pressed a kiss to his lips. "It does sound better when you say it."

Chay smiled, and then a lighter contraction hit.

"Afterbirth." Nilo said. "Koren, finish cleaning up the babies and get them swaddled. We should be done here soon."

An hour later, Koren sat with both babies in his arms. Pride and love lit his eyes, and he gazed at Chay. "I know I've said it before, but thank you for this. I love you so much."

Chay smiled sleepily. "And I love you."

A knock sounded at the door. Koren sighed. "I think we have to let people in."

"Yeah. We do. Think about this every time you get the urge to have more kids."

Laughing, Koren called for their friends and family to come in and meet the babies.

About A. J. Stone

A.J. Stone loves rainbows and bears. Visit http://www.michelezurloauthor.com/a.j.-stone.html for the latest information or follow A.J. Stone on Facebook at https://www.facebook.com/AJStoneBearsCove/ to keep up with the newest releases, and feel free to request stories for your favorite Bear's Cove characters.

Reviews let A.J. know you want more!

Bear's Cove Series (MM/MPreg) by A. J. Stone
Dak's Omega
Tanzil's Second Chance
Perfect Blend: Kofi's Omega

Draco International Series (MM/MPreg) by A. J. Stone
Amaricio's Omega Shifter
Koren's Omega Neighbor
Zeke's Reluctant Omega

MM Romance by Nicoline Tiernan
Nexus #1: Tristan's Lover by Nicoline Tiernan
Nexus #2: The Man of His Dreams by Nicoline Tiernan

Sneak Peek at Zeke's Reluctant Omega (Draco International 3)

A half hour later, Zeke signed into the hospital as a visitor, and he found Mr. Yardan's room without incident. He'd been admitted to a short-term observation unit, which meant they weren't sure as to the extent of his injuries. After a brief knock on the open door, he entered the room. Seeing the man propped up against the raised back of the bed sent a shockwave through Zeke's body.

It wasn't the large bandages that covered the side of his head and his exposed shoulder or the splint on his arm that caused any kind of reaction. Zeke had been through enough battles to have seen every kind of wound imaginable, as well as a few that were difficult to conceive. No, this was a shock of awareness on the part of his dragon, and he'd never before felt anything like it.

Caught by surprise at this new, surreal feeling, Zeke found himself momentarily dumbstruck. His dragon came to the fore, exercising dominion by sharpening his senses. He noted the damages, sensing the concussion, broken bones, multiple contusions, and the tender ankle. Simultaneously he took in the long, sinewy muscles that the shapeless hospital gown and the blanket draped over his legs couldn't quite camouflage.

He had a powerful urge to taste Marcel Yardan. He wanted to know the exact flavor of his kiss, his dark chocolate skin, and his seed. His dragon purred insistently, demanding a sample, and Zeke had every intention of indulging it.

"You're not the doctor."

The voice jerked Zeke from the primal reverie that had overtaken him. He glanced to his left to find a man seated in a chair next to the bed. With his highlighted blond hair and cornflower blue eyes to bring out his handsomeness, and a ripped body to match, this man qualified as a potential impediment to Zeke's claiming of his mate.

That man had noted his non-medical status.

Zeke drew himself up, puffing out his chest to appear even larger. "You're not the patient."

The guy's gaze wandered Zeke's body. "You're not a relative, either."

Gritting his teeth, Zeke threw the observation back. "Nor are you."

"Friend," the blond said. He looked to Marcel. "You know this guy?"

Marcel seemed dazed. He stared at Zeke. After a long time, a response croaked from his throat. "No."

Zeke reached toward the tray next to the bed. "You need water." He held the cup to Marcel's lips while the potential omega sipped.

After a bit, Marcel leaned back. "Thank you. I didn't catch your name or why you're here."

"Ezekiel Lowry, but my friends call me Zeke."

Marcel offered his hand. "I'm Marcel, and this is my friend, Holden."

The first contact of skin sent a jolt of electricity and need through Zeke, and it left Marcel with a more confused wrinkle to his lovely chin. "I'm the Head of Security for Draco International."

"Oh," Holden gasped. "You're from the theater?"

A bit of Marcel's confusion leaped to Zeke. "Theater?"

Holden sat up straighter and clasped his hands in front of his chest. "The Verdance Theater. Draco International is a major sponsor of the arts. They have the biggest banners in the lobby."

Zeke shrugged. Amar would know more about where DI spent their money. "I'm in security, not philanthropy."

"Mr. Lowry, why are you here?" Marcel asked.

It bothered Zeke that Marcel didn't treat him with familiarity. He didn't want any barriers of propriety standing between them. He considered Holden, and all the ways in which he was an impediment. "Holden, can you step out into the hall and give us a moment?"

Holden, to his credit, looked to Marcel to see what he wanted.

Marcel pressed his luscious lips together, no doubt waging an internal struggle between unexplained urges and his better sense. Zeke recognized this because he was also navigating those turbulent waters.

Finally, he shook his head, a tiny movement that ran counter to what his animal wanted. Zeke assumed that Marcel was a shifter because, otherwise, why would his dragon be so insistent? Marcel ran his tongue along his luscious lower lip. "Holden stays."

Zeke motioned to an unoccupied chair. "Mind if I sit?"

"Knock yourself out." Marcel watched, half wary and half curious, as Zeke slid a heavy chair closer and sat down.